"I haven't thanked y[...]

Chloe glanced at the stern man bes[...] he hadn't asked her to accompany him; he'd [...] hurried her outside and bundled her into [...] s if he had every right.

"No problem."

"But I'm sure it was. You didn't have to wait, you know. I could have called a cab."

He didn't bother to respond.

Mr. Y ignored the hostage beside him as if he knew she hadn't the strength to try to escape. Time was of the essence. He had to get her out of town before...

"This isn't the way to my car."

"That's right."

"Do you mind my asking where you're taking me?"

To a woodcutter's hut deep in the Carpathian Mountains, replied the infamous Mr. Y. Once I have the formula in hand, you'll be led back to the village unharmed—blindfolded, of course.

"My house," answered her captor.

Or rescuer—Chloe didn't quite know which. Lord, she had to quit playing mind games and start getting organized again! This was no spy novel. This was reality. Sooner or later, she was going to have to deal with it....

Dear Reader,

In September, we've got an extra special surprise for you! There's been so much enthusiasm for our DIAMOND JUBILEE titles, that this month we've got two DIAMOND JUBILEE books for you by two of your favorite authors: Annette Broadrick with *Married?!* and Dixie Browning with *The Homing Instinct*.

The DIAMOND JUBILEE—Silhouette Romance's tenth anniversary celebration—is our way of saying thanks to you, our readers. To symbolize the timelessness of love, as well as the modern gift of the tenth anniversary, we're presenting readers with a DIAMOND JUBILEE Silhouette Romance each month, penned by one of your favorite Silhouette Romance authors. In the coming months, writers such as Stella Bagwell, Lucy Gordon and Phyllis Halldorson are writing DIAMOND JUBILEE titles especially for you.

And that's not all! There are six books a month from Silhouette Romance—stories by wonderful writers who time and time again bring home the magic of love. During our anniversary year, each book is special and written with romance in mind. September brings you *Romeo in the Rain* by Kasey Michaels—a sequel to her heart-warming *His Chariot Awaits*. And in the coming months works by such loved writers as Diana Palmer, Brittany Young and Victoria Glenn are sure to put a smile on your lips.

During our tenth anniversary, the spirit of celebration is with us year-round. And that's all due to you, our readers. With the support you've given us, you can look forward to many more years of heartwarming, poignant love stories.

I hope you'll enjoy this book and all of the stories to come. Come home to romance—Silhouette Romance—for always!

Sincerely,

Tara Hughes Gavin
Senior Editor

DIXIE BROWNING

The Homing Instinct

Published by Silhouette Books New York

America's Publisher of Contemporary Romance

SILHOUETTE BOOKS
300 E. 42nd St., New York, N.Y. 10017

ISBN: 0-373-08747-0

First Silhouette Books printing September 1990

Printed in the U.S.A.

Books by Dixie Browning

_____

DIXIE BROWNING

has written over forty books for Silhouette since 1980. She is a charter member of the Romance Writers of America, and *Renegade Player* won an RWA Golden Medallion. Along with her writing, Dixie has been acclaimed as a watercolor painter, and was the first president of the Watercolor Society of North Carolina. She is currently president of Browning Artworks, Ltd., a gallery featuring fine crafts on Hatteras Island.

A letter to my friends

Has it been ten years since Silhouette was born? Strange . . . I don't feel ten years older, but I suppose I must be. Isn't it funny how things change and yet remain the same?

Remember all those virginal young heroines who were so dreadfully vulnerable, always at the mercy of cruel fate and some arrogant, gray-templed hero who covered a micron of warmth with a hundred and fifty pounds of stainless steel?

I loved them, didn't you? Beauty and the beast, and we know who always won.

As writers, we've been allowed to grow with the times, to reflect the changes in our society, for better or for worse. And we've done it, I hope, without ever losing sight of why we have always responded to romance, both as readers and as women.

For the core truth never changes—man is by nature an undomesticated beast. If civilization is to go forward, it's up to women to change that.

And thereby, dear friend, hangs many a tale. . . .

All the best,

Dixie Browning

Chapter One

What *was* the number of this highway, anyhow? Did it even have a number? If Chloe had seen it, she'd already forgotten it—which was probably not too surprising. After hurriedly packing and clearing up all the ragtag ends yesterday, then driving seven hours and sleeping for perhaps two on the rock-hard motel bed last night, it was no wonder she was going road blind.

At least she was still headed roughly north, away from Florida. Hopefully Keedysville would be distant enough and small enough that no one would look at her face and frown, as if to say "Where have I seen *you* before?"

Or, if they heard her name, they still wouldn't know.

Indulging in an old favorite pastime, Chloe imagined the waitress at the motel restaurant, who had served her coffee and toast along with curious looks and some leading questions. *"Baskin?" The waitress shifted her weight to one hip while she squinted up at the water-stained ceiling. "Baskin, Baskin... Oh yeah, sure! The ice-cream people, right? You one o' them Baskins?"*

She wasn't. Besides, she'd signed the register as C. B. Palmer.

"Palmer? You mean like that baseball guy, the one that models men's briefs? If it's models you're looking for, my sister's boy..."

A wintry smile flickered briefly in Chloe's large gray-green eyes, like a momentary flash of sunlight after a Hobe Sound squall. As long as she was "creating" why not create herself a different name? Like Smith. Or Jones. And a different face.

And a different past....

Chloe had left I-95 somewhere in Georgia and followed secondary roads since then. No particular order, just so long as they took her generally north, and eventually to the small Maryland town where her only remaining relative lived.

She had set out after lunch today on Highway 17, and then cut over onto something even smaller. It was much less traveled, which had suited her just fine. But now, with the sun setting behind her, she was beginning to wonder if she hadn't made a mistake. Lunch had been three bites of a dry hamburger and three cups of weak coffee. She was tired and hungry, and for the first time in ages she'd been actually looking forward to her next meal, but all she'd seen since she turned off Highway 17 onto this glorified cow-path were pine trees, canals, and wet fields that seemed to stretch out forever.

The car ahead of her maintained a steady fifty-four miles an hour. They were the only two vehicles on the road, now that the logging truck had turned off. It was dark gray—expensive, but not flashy. Just the opposite, in fact. As tired as she was, Chloe found her mind wandering again. "Hiding from reality," her father used to call it. She'd been making up stories in her mind since she was a child—first about stray animals, then, as she grew older, about strangers glimpsed in passing, fragments of conversation overheard in a crowd.

Besides, she had to do something to combat the monotony of mile after featureless mile of blacktop. As tired as she was, it would be all too easy to fall asleep at the wheel, and while she was admittedly running away, she had no intention of taking *that* particular way out. One in the family was enough.

Gripping the wheel until her knuckles whitened, Chloe forced her mind to release the past. Studying the car ahead, she spoke aloud. "All right, Palmer, it's a dark and stormy night, and we have our subject under surveillance. What do we know about him? His name?"

His name. The mystery man had to have a name.

Again Chloe nearly smiled. Myster-Y, of course. Mister Y.

And already she knew that Mr. Y was an excellent if somewhat conservative driver. She watched as he skillfully straddled a large snake that had slithered onto the highway. Without conscious thought, she followed his example, her mind caught up in her story.

He was a highly successful...what? Race-car driver? Hardly. Soldier of fortune? Wrong clothes, wrong vehicle, wrong—everything.

Actually, all she could discern from her particular vantage point was a pair of broad, square shoulders in what appeared to be a well-cut suit, and a nicely shaped head—dark hair, rather thick.

Ears? Definitely visible, but not too prominent.

Posture? Superb. Possibly even military. But what would a military man be doing here in the middle of nowhere on a late Thursday afternoon in November?

Well, he was on a secret mission, of course. Had to be. Thus the anonymous but powerful-looking automobile. Peddling a secret soybean fertilizer formula to the Ukrainians, probably.

Just at that moment, Mr. Y turned to watch a hawk lift off from a dead pine beside the highway, and Chloe caught a glimpse of his profile, which only confirmed her opinion. He had the profile of a secret agent. Not young, but not old, either. And definitely not "anonymous." Those were suspiciously Slavic-looking cheekbones—and was that a mustache under his jutting nose, or just a shadow?

She was still pondering the possibility of a mustache—probably fake—when he turned to face forward again, which might explain why she didn't see the buck until he'd leaped across the ditch and was all but mounted on the hood of her car.

With reflexes honed by years of childhood tennis lessons, Chloe managed to wrench the wheel to the right in time to miss the animal's haunches by a hair.

But there was no way on God's green earth she could avoid the lone pine tree growing on the bank of the drainage canal.

Quinton Stevens was running late. It wasn't every evening that a man celebrated his own engagement, and though he wasn't looking forward to it, he'd promised Janet he'd be back in plenty of time.

His mind on the tentative agreement he'd just reached to build a planned community, including a small shopping center, for a Greenville consortium, he'd been aware of the silver Mercedes behind him ever since he'd turned off 17. He wished to hell the woman would get off his tail and pass him—he'd deliberately dropped his speed so that she could—but he wasn't going to slow down to a turtle's pace, not with Janet expecting him at her house in less than two hours.

Raking his late-day stubble, Quint glanced in the rearview mirror just as the eight-point buck hurtled across the highway behind him.

What the hell—!

He had braked, switched off the engine and was out of his own car before the one behind him had quite finished settling against the pine. Even as he watched, its rear end began to slide slowly down the bank toward the ditch.

Acting automatically, he snatched up a fallen branch and jammed it, butt forward, under the right rear wheel, which slowed up the slide enough for him to get the chocks out of his own trunk and ram them in place.

Having learned to drive some twenty-five years ago on logging roads, construction sites and along the miles of unpaved highway in northeastern North Carolina, Quint made it a practice to carry a tow rope, traction mats, chocks and jumper cables at all times.

The woman behind the wheel was belted in, thank God. She was as white as a sheet now, and she'd be sore as hell come morning, but at least she was still alive.

"Okay, okay, take it easy now," he murmured, opening her door. These babies were built to protect the driver, but she wasn't going to be really happy about the condition of her front end once she pulled herself together enough to climb out. He reached past her and switched off the ignition. Straining to wedge his shoulders out again without touching her, he breathed in deeply. He was profoundly grateful to smell only leather and some subtle perfume that reminded him of his mother's flower garden—not blood, smoke and gasoline.

"Give it a minute more—don't try to move yet," he said.

"I—didn't hit him, did I?"

"Who, the buck? No, he made it okay, but you sure didn't do that pine tree much good. Scared it out of a dozen growth rings." Come on, lady, lighten up, he willed. Don't fall apart on me now!

Quint shook his head. She looked about as substantial as a shadow on a fog bank. Spacey. He'd better quit trying to bring her around with bad jokes and just get her the hell out of there before she passed out on him.

Reaching around her again, he unfastened her seat belt. "You feel steady enough to try getting out now?" he asked, extending his arms.

"Thank you. I'm fine."

Her voice said one thing; his ears heard another. She was in shock, but he didn't think she was badly injured. From what he could see, she hadn't struck anything. Still, you never could tell. The belt might not have been tight enough. Some women wore them loose for comfort. She could have cracked the steering wheel with her...

His dark gaze dropped briefly to her breasts and then moved away. One thing about it—a woman who drove a Mercedes and wore clothes like that wasn't used to sitting around on ditch banks passing the time of day with strange men. The sooner he got her out of here, the sooner he could be on his way.

"Relax now, ma'am. I've got you— No, dammit. Don't wriggle! I've got the door jammed open, but the way she's tilted, things might start to shift any minute."

The hand that clutched at his was long, soft and trembling. She wasn't wearing any rings. In fact she wasn't wearing any jewelry at all, as far as he could see—not even a watch.

Probably allergic to metal. He had a cousin like that. Loved gold, could afford to buy it by the pound, but one touch and she broke out in great welts. "My car," she began as he carried her carefully to his.

"Don't worry about it now. Let's get you settled first, and I'll drive you into Williamston to the hospital. You just relax, Miss...Mrs.—"

"Palmer," she answered, in a voice that reminded him of watered-down tea. Elegant, but too thin for his taste.

Come to think of it, that was a pretty fair description of the woman herself. Elegant, but too thin for his taste. Janet would make two of her. Not that Janet was what you might call heavy. She was just... sturdier.

"Okay, Miz Palmer," he continued in what he hoped was a reassuring tone, but which sounded more like a gravel mixer, even to his own ears. "You just close your eyes and I'll get you to the emergency room in no time. You'll be in good hands. Relax—try not to worry."

He maintained a steady speed, about five miles over the limit, and Chloe drew in a deep, shuddering breath and expelled it sharply. She closed her eyes and tried to force herself to relax. Not to worry? The man didn't look like a fool, but looks could be deceiving. "About my car," she said, inhaling deeply again. "Do you think—is it—?"

"Totalled?" he rumbled, in a cross between a drawl and a growl. "No, I don't think so. Lost a fender, grill—possibly a radiator—but the frame's probably all right. From the skid marks, I'd say you'd lost a lot of momentum before you hit."

She couldn't even remember using the brakes. Fortunately, some things were instinctive.

"Are you too cold? Too warm?" He adjusted the temperature, opened the vent and angled it so that it blew in her face.

"I'm not going to faint," she announced more firmly, closing the vent.

"Thank God for that," he replied under his breath. A farm truck entered the highway ahead of him, and he waited for a chance and passed it.

With another deep sigh—she seemed to want to gulp in air for some reason—Chloe closed her eyes again. Oddly enough, she trusted him. Mr. Y was an excellent driver. His dossier said so. She should know, shouldn't she? She'd created him.

And she'd been right about the mustache and the Slavic cheekbones.

Traffic picked up considerably, and she watched with a total lack of interest as they approached a small town.

"Be there in half a minute," he reassured her.

Be where? Oh yes—the hospital. But she didn't need a hospital. All she needed was a place to lie down for five minutes so that she could catch her breath before she started calling garages about her car. Still, he had to take her somewhere, she supposed.

"Really, you've been more than kind," she murmured, but he was busy maneuvering between an ambulance and a pickup truck.

Almost before they got inside, the questions began. Chloe started shaking again. She clutched Quint's arm. Questions. Oh, God, not more questions! That was why she'd left in the first place.

A nurse met them just inside the door and, after a single sharp look at them both, took her arm and began to lead her away. Quint took two steps to follow and then stopped, staring after them. She looked back at him once, and the expression on her face hit him where he lived. He wanted to run.

He didn't. For reasons he didn't bother to examine, he stayed rooted to the spot, watching as the tall, thin woman with the long, dark blond hair that was beginning to uncoil down over her stiffly held shoulders, was led down the corridor.

Other than the fact that her lean, high-browed face was the color of wet plaster, she looked like a mannequin in a high-class store window. Pale gray suit a size too large, white silk blouse, ditto, gray snakeskin shoes and pale stockings on a pair of legs that...

He had to admit that, skinny or not, those legs of hers were extraordinary. Not a straight line on 'em anywhere. One subtle curve flowed into another until they disappeared up under her—

Quint cleared his throat and glared at a No-Smoking sign. Okay, Stevens, you've done your duty, he told himself sternly. You brought her in, but strictly speaking, you're not involved. She's of age and fully conscious. She can take it from here.

But could she?

He frowned and looked around for a coffee machine. There was always one around a waiting room somewhere....

Her purse. She'd need that, and she hadn't had it with her when the nurse had led her away. He remembered collecting it, and—what?

Tossing it into the back seat, along with her luggage.

It took less than three minutes to retrieve the small gray snakeskin bag. He was standing in the middle of the empty waiting room clutching the thing in both hands when a nurse who introduced herself as Amelia Biggs appeared at his side, saying, "If you don't mind, sir, I need to ask you some questions?"

"Ask away ma'am, but I doubt if I can be any help. I never met the lady before she tackled that pine tree."

"You were involved?"

"No, I'm only a witness. I happened to see this eight-pointer run out in front of her—saw her swerve. Naturally, I brought her in—her car's a mess."

Ms. Biggs looked pointedly at the small gray purse clutched incongruously in his large, work-hardened hands. "Would you mind giving me her full name, age, social security number, address, and the name of her next of kin?"

Quint felt a film of cold sweat break out on his forehead. He thrust the bag at the nurse and said, "She's not—? That is, she's going to—? Oh, hell, I've gotta get out of here!"

She stopped him before he made it to the door. "Sir, your friend's going to be all right, only she refuses to talk. She clams right up when we ask her anything. Do you know if she happened to hit her head?"

Feeling a bit queasy himself, Quint told the woman he didn't think so. "She was belted in. Look, like I said, I don't even know the lady. Why don't you just take a look inside her purse." He tried once more to hand it over, to no avail. "If she won't talk, you can probably find all you need in here."

"Oh, no. I can't do that, sir. It's against hospital policy."

"Well, hell, I'm not about to go pawing through some strange woman's personal belongings the minute her back's turned. Her name's Palmer, if that's any help to you. She had Florida plates."

But in the end, it was Quint who opened the purse and took inventory. He was rather surprised to see how little there was to find. He'd always thought women carried at least half their worldly possessions in those dinky things. Janet normally used her brief-case instead of a purse.

"One scarf, silk," he muttered. He could tell that much by the feel. "One lipstick, black and gold." At least the case was. "One pen, fountain type, tortoise-shell and gold. One comb, tortoiseshell with gold trim. A pair of sunglasses that looked as if they might be prescription. Tortoiseshell frames. One, ah . . ." He examined the article in question, frowning.

"Compact," Amelia Biggs supplied, and he nod-ded and dropped it back into the bag.

"And one billfold, gray—uh—ostrich, gold clasp."

While Biggs looked on, he reluctantly opened the billfold. "One driver's license, name of Chloe Baskin Palmer, age—hmm—thirty-three." The picture didn't do her justice. Didn't the woman ever smile?

He handed the laminated card over. "Here, you can copy off the address and whatever else you need."

"That's it?"

He flipped through the compartments and came up with nothing. Zilch. "That's it. Sorry."

"No insurance card?"

He shook his head. Amelia Biggs's already thin lips disappeared altogether. He didn't bother to restate the obvious—that there were no credit cards, no bank card, no checkbook—and unless he'd overlooked a secret compartment somewhere, the woman had ex-actly ninety-seven dollars and some odd cents. Hardly enough to cover extensive medical costs, not to mention the repairs on a Mercedes 380SL.

Biggs marched off, the purse in hand, and Quint told himself he needed to get out of there. Even if he took the unpaved shortcut, he was still some thirty-seven minutes away from home. And Janet's party—his own damned engagement party—was due to get under way in about fifteen minutes, give or take a few seconds.

Janet was a stickler for punctuality. She was dependable, responsible and punctual. Those were the very things he liked best about her.

But before he could make up his mind to leave, a young intern came out of the examining room and approached him. "You brought Mrs. Palmer in, I understand?"

Quint nodded, not wanting to hear what he suspected he was about to hear.

"She's fine," the young man said, and Quint felt for the wall behind him and leaned against it.

"You're sure?" *You're sure the contents of her billfold didn't affect the outcome of her examination, you jerk?*

"Well, she's shaken, of course. Some bruises—she'll have a big one on her left clavicle, but other than those and the stiffness, which'll probably peak in a couple of days, I don't anticipate any problems. You can take her home now, if you want to. She's getting dressed. Be out in a minute."

And while Quint was still digesting that particular development, the intern continued, "Why don't you stop by Admissions and clear up a few things with them while you wait? It's two doors down on your right."

Thus it was that Chloe found herself being bundled back into the front seat of the dark gray sedan with a perfect stranger. It was now completely dark, and she was feeling slightly sick to her stomach, which was probably no more than hunger, she told herself.

She glanced at the stern man beside her. He hadn't asked her to accompany him; he'd merely hurried her outside and bundled her into his car as if he had every right. "I haven't thanked you," she murmured.

"No problem."

"But I'm sure it was. You didn't have to wait, you know. I could have called a cab."

He didn't bother to respond.

Mr. Y ignored the hostage beside him as if he knew she hadn't the strength to try to escape. Time was of the essence. He had to get her out of town before...

"This isn't the way to my car."

"That's right."

"Do you mind my asking where you're taking me?"

"To a woodcutter's hut, deep in the Carpathian Mountains," replied the infamous Mr. Y. "Once I have the formula in hand, you'll be led back to the village unharmed—blindfolded, of course."

"My house," answered her captor.

Or rescuer—Chloe didn't quite know which. God, she had to quit playing mind games and start getting organized again! This was no spy novel. This was reality. Sooner or later, she was going to have to deal with it. "Why your house?" she demanded.

"Why? Because at the moment, I don't have time to drive you around until you locate a motel that suits you, and the garage won't be doing anything about your car until tomorrow, anyway, and besides—"

"But I can't just leave it out there. What if someone comes along and steals it?"

"How many thieves do you know who drive a tow truck?"

"I don't know any thieves," she replied, and then quickly averted her face.

But not before Quint had seen her stricken look. Seen it and wondered about it. "Lucky you," he remarked dryly. "Well, folks around here are a pretty honest bunch, so I wouldn't worry about it." He shifted in his seat without slackening his speed, and dug a set of car keys out of his pocket—*her* car keys. "Here you go, Miz Palmer. I locked it before we left. But like I said, I don't think you'll have to worry between now and morning."

Chloe accepted the keys and clutched them until they bit into her tender palms. After two or three deep breaths—the intern had warned her about hyperventilating—she said quietly, "I don't even know your name."

"Quinton Stevens."

When no more was forthcoming, she told him, "I don't know why you're being so kind to me, but I do appreciate it. I'll be glad to pay you for the time and expense involved."

"Like you paid the hospital?"

Her head fell back against the headrest, and she groaned. "Oh, no. . . I forgot all about that. They'll send me a bill, won't they?"

"At your Tallahassee address?"

"No, at my Hobe Sound— How did you know?"

"Lady, if you didn't hit your head, I hope to God you have some other excuse. You aren't fit to be running around loose."

"How did you know my address?"

"From your driver's license, remember? You wouldn't talk, so somebody had to do the honors. I gave them your driver's license. Didn't they give it back?"

"Oh . . . yes, of course. I'm sorry, I wasn't thinking. But about their bill, it might be—ah, some time before I go home again."

"You left a forwarding address?"

It was none of his business, but Chloe had been too well brought up to remind him of that fact. While she was thinking of an answer, he said, "Yeah, well . . . never mind. I paid the tab."

If possible, that made her feel even worse than she felt already. Nervously snapping and unsnapping the magnetic catch on her purse, she stared ahead, watching the occasional white farmhouse glimmer past in the dark. "There are a lot of trees here, aren't there?"

He grunted an unintelligible response.

After a while, she tried again. Silence was a vacuum that filled too quickly with thoughts, and at the moment, she didn't want to think. *"I'll think about that tomorrow."* Or better yet: *"Frankly, Quinton, I don't give a damn."* "Is it far? To your house, I mean?"

"Not too much farther."

Which could mean anything from half a mile to a hundred. "I really don't mind going to a hotel. I'm not at all particular, honestly. Even a motel would be just lovely."

"Mmm-hmm."

"You've done so much already, Mr. Stevens. Of course, I'll reimburse you for everything, but I do hate to impose on your hospitality. Unexpected guests—"

"Hardly unexpected, since I'm bringing you with me."

"But your family—"

"Look, if it'll make you feel any better, ma'am, I live alone in a nine-room house, and the nearest neighbor lives about a mile away, down a logging road. So you're not going to be imposing on anyone, okay?"

Chloe sat up straight, her tired eyes widening in a pale face. Was that supposed to be reassuring? She was streaking off through the night with a perfect stranger who admitted to living miles away from civilization—if not to being a Ukrainian fertilizer spy—and she was supposed to feel *comforted*?

"Thank you," she replied with a spark of spirit that had not surfaced in recent years. "I feel immeasurably better, knowing that."

Chapter Two

Except for the occasional deep, shuddering sigh, Chloe remained silent until they pulled up beside a pale, two-story frame house shadowed by a deep front porch. A yard light shone on several outbuildings, and from somewhere nearby came the soft low murmur of a dove—or possibly an owl.

Quinton stopped the car beside the house and helped her out as if she were an invalid. "I'm sure this is an imposition," she murmured as he led her carefully up the steps and onto the porch.

"No problem." He unlocked the door and held it wide for her to enter. "Uh—there's this—that is, I'm going to have to leave you alone for a while this evening, but—"

"Oh, please! Don't let me be a bother. Go right ahead with your plans. I'll be fine if I can just lie down for a few minutes."

She looked up at him—rather a long way up, because Quinton Stevens topped her own five foot nine by at least five inches. Thanks to his deep chest and broad shoulders, his height had not been all that obvious, but suddenly she was struck by the fact that her Mister Y was a remarkably attractive man, furrowed brow and tired eyes notwithstanding.

This is absurd, Chloe told herself. I know I haven't been thinking too clearly lately, but this is totally absurd!

"Did you eat supper?" Quinton frowned and then answered his own question. "No, of course not. I'll make you a sandwich while you get settled in. I put your bag in my trunk—you go on upstairs and find a room that suits you, and I'll bring it up. Then I'll see about getting you something to eat. My room's the one at the front of the house. Help yourself to the rest. Bathroom's second door on the right."

"Please, I can't let you waste any more time on my behalf. You've been so kind, but I know you have other things to do." The last thing she wanted was to get involved with anyone, even to the extent of accepting a night's hospitality. She should have stayed with her car and asked him to send the highway patrol—then she might have retained a modicum of control over the situation.

"Mrs. Palmer, I'm not about to waste my time on anyone, but you need food and a place to sleep, and I have both. Look, I'll fetch your bag and throw together a sandwich, and then I'll leave you to get some rest. Come morning, we can sort it all out." Chloe tried to interrupt, but he barreled right over her as if she hadn't opened her mouth. "Right now, you're in no shape to do much of anything, and like I said, I'm running late for my own engagement party, so be a nice lady and don't hassle me, okay?''

When he put it that way, what choice did she have? Assertiveness had never been her long suit. At the moment, she lacked the gumption to swat a fly, much less to tackle a giant with a granite jaw and a pair of chocolate-colored eyes that were bittersweet, at best.

At any rate, the man had shown her nothing but kindness. It had been a long time since anyone had been kind to her with no thought of getting something in return.

In less time than she would have thought possible, Chloe found herself settled into a chilly, musty-smelling bedroom with rose-sprigged wallpaper, an ivory-painted iron bed, and a handsome, if dusty, golden oak washstand. The other rooms had been even dustier and mustier.

''Bed's probably not made up,'' Quinton apologized. ''But if you don't mind—''

''Of course I don't mind,'' she hastened to assure him, wondering if she could summon up the strength to fold back a bedspread. Make her own bed? She might just collapse in a heap on the floor.

''I'd do it for you, but—''

She managed a creditable smile. ''I know—you're late for your own engagement party. Please don't bother. I'll be just fine.''

''Linen closet's across there.'' He pointed a square-tipped forefinger to a small door at the end of the hall. ''Help yourself.''

Ten minutes later, Chloe had managed to smooth a pair of crisp, faintly yellowed sheets on to the mattress. She'd located a wool blanket that smelled of mothballs and hoped it would be sufficient.

When Quint appeared at the door with a steaming cup of coffee and a thick, untidy sandwich on a paper plate, she was seated in a bentwood rocker, her hands clasped in her lap, wondering if she'd completely taken leave of her senses.

The man was a perfect stranger! She had allowed him to lead her around like a dog on a leash, when all she knew about him was his name and the fact that he was in the process of getting himself engaged.

Which was some protection, after all, she supposed. A man on the verge of marriage would scarcely be a threat to another woman. Still, she didn't even know the name of the town where he lived, or even if it qualified as a town.

"There's a phone in the hall you're welcome to use if you want to make a call."

"Thank you, but that won't be necessary." He had already told her nothing could be done about her car until morning. As tired as she was, she was willing to leave it at that.

"Sure you don't want to let someone know where you are?"

"That really won't be necessary, thank you." Ginny wouldn't be expecting her. The invitation issued two months ago at her father's funeral, while sincere, had been casual and open-ended, with no dates mentioned. And other than Ginny, there was no one.

He hesitated a moment, a slight frown forming as he studied her pale features. "Then let me give you the number where I can be reached." Tearing a corner off a notepad on the hall table, he scribbled down a number and handed the scrap to her. "There's plenty more sandwich makings, and I made a full pot of coffee. You'd probably be better off drinking milk, though."

Already having sampled his coffee, Chloe silently agreed with him. His idea of coffee was her idea of paint remover. "Thank you," she said for the hundredth time. Why couldn't he just go? She needed to think, and her mind refused to function with him looking at her like that. The man was entirely too big. She could have sworn that he used up more than his share of oxygen in the room.

Yet, after he'd gone, she felt like calling him back. As big as he was—as intimidating in his clumsily kind way—she felt terribly alone without him.

Setting the uncomfortable rocker in motion, she clutched the large mug and stared unseeingly at the ivory-painted door that had closed behind him. Slowly a slice of cheese slithered out of her sandwich and landed in her lap, and with a sigh, she tucked it back in and began to eat.

Quint would have given a lot to know whether or not Chloe B. Palmer was going to place a call, and if so, to whom. He was somewhat surprised at his own curiosity. The woman meant nothing at all to him. He'd taken her home with him because it had been the quickest and easiest thing to do—short of dropping her on a street corner.

What did he know about her? Nothing. She was from Florida, evidently with more than one address. She was well-heeled, even though she carried little money on her. She was as closemouthed as a skink, and had a way of moving that could elevate the blood pressure of a corpse—if the corpse happened to be male.

And he was spending altogether too much time and energy trying to wedge a crack in the invisible wall that surrounded her, he thought angrily.

Janet. He'd better start psyching himself up for this party of hers. He hadn't wanted it, but Janet had thought it would be a smart move. She had invited a few relatives—her lawyer brother and sister-in-law, whom he had never particularly liked, and two of Quint's male cousins and their wives. Other than a handful of mutual friends, the rest were all business associates.

The party would be a tax write-off—a business expense, Janet had claimed—and although he wasn't the least bit sentimental, that had struck a sour note with him. God knows, this was no love match. They were both approaching middle age, both alone. Janet had had one love affair that had ended badly, and now she was looking for a good excuse to get away from her domineering mother.

As for him—he'd had Janet's younger sister, Marissa. Almost.

He'd have to hand it to her—Janet was a smart woman. Her brother Gerald had been dead set on going to law school, so it was Janet who had grown up in their families' joint real-estate business. When she'd inherited her father's forty-nine percent of the stock, she had been determined to concentrate on commercial rather than residential development.

Quint had quietly stood fast. His parents had been killed in an auto accident almost fifteen years before, which left him his father's fifty-one percent of the business. Like his father, Quint preferred residential development to commercial, although the firm did both. Personally, he liked the idea of creating homes for families—well-planned houses on well-chosen terrain, buildings that would grow lovelier through the years instead of becoming obsolete, as so much commercial development did.

He had never enjoyed the battles that all too often accompanied commercial development—battles with zoning boards and irate citizens' groups opposed to the intrusion of business into their quiet residential neighborhoods. In Vietnam he'd seen enough of war to last him several lifetimes.

But Janet thrived on confrontation, going after commercial development with a single-mindedness that amazed him. She enjoyed a good fight. This was one of the many areas in which they differed.

He sighed, suddenly feeling the weight of a day that had begun well before dawn. Sooner or later he was going to have to take a few days off—or even a few hours. There had to be something in life besides work.

By the time Quint pulled into the neo-Colonial mansion where Janet lived with her widowed mother, he was a good hour-and-a-half late. He'd called from home to let her know he hadn't skipped the country, but he felt like a heel, even so.

Dammit, Janet deserved better treatment. She worked sixty hour weeks for the firm. She never complained when he was too tired to take her out—matter of fact, she was too tired about as often as he was. And she didn't expect romance from a guy who was pushing forty and had never claimed to love her as more than a friend. In fact, it was a toss-up as to which one of them would be the more embarrassed by any such display of emotion.

They were both realists, which was why this marriage stood a pretty fair chance of surviving. According to Janet, whose idea it had been in the first place, it would ensure that there'd be no disruption in the business such as could occur if one or the other of them married an outsider.

Not that either of them had anyone else in mind; nor were they likely to at their ages. They'd known each other all their lives, and they got along like two peas in a pod.

Janet greeted him at the door, looking attractive in a blue wool dress that complemented her brown hair and pale blue eyes. "You look like you could do with a drink, Quint. How'd everything go in Greenville?"

"Looks promising. The backing's sound enough, the land's excellent—no drainage problems, good demographics. Sorry I'm late, but it couldn't be helped."

"No problem. You always were one to drag home every stray in the woods. Is she going to be all right?"

It occurred to Quint that another woman might show some small sign of jealousy under the circumstances. Janet barely even showed a trace of curiosity. Not for the first time, he wondered if they were being entirely wise. A vision arose in his mind of himself growing stooped and gray, his mind dulled by boredom, and he deliberately shut it out.

"Hmm? Oh, yeah—she'll be fine. Just needs some time to see about getting her car fixed. I'll call Buster in the morning."

"Tell him to put a rush on it. He owes you one for getting him square with the zoning board. I'd better circulate now, but you can stick around after everybody leaves and fill me in on the details. I checked out this Greenville bunch. You're right—if they're backing it, there won't be any trouble. Old tobacco money.''

Two men in dark business suits waved Janet over, and she smiled over her shoulder as she hurried away. "Get a drink and come talk to Adamson. I think you might be interested in what he's got in mind."

Quint helped himself to a tonic and lime. He was too tired to risk anything stronger. But instead of joining Janet and the two men she was with, he strolled over to the fireplace, which contained a basket of chrysanthemums instead of glowing coals, and gazed out over the large, handsomely appointed room.

There were half a dozen women present—mostly relatives—and some two dozen or so men. Janet had always felt more comfortable with men, claiming that women bored her, with their talk of children and clothes and recipes. She often bragged that she thought like a man, and for the first time, Quinton wondered if that was such a great thing, after all.

Chloe alternately slept and worried. The doctor had given her something to calm her nerves, but she hadn't taken it. After Quint's coffee, she needed it more than ever, but she dared not risk taking anything that might prevent her from thinking clearly.

As if thinking clearly were even a remote possibility.

It had been this way for months. Actually, it had started years ago, back when she'd first begun to suspect that her marriage wasn't made in heaven.

Quite the contrary. As she'd eventually learned, it had been made in her father's study—a deal between him, a prominent banker who was a powerful behind-the-scenes influence in politics, and an up-and-coming young lawyer with political ambitions. The deal had been consummated a few years later, when Chloe had graduated from Hollins and returned to Hobe Sound, where her father was living with wife number three.

Tall, gawky and congenitally shy—that had been her father's favorite description of her. Quite naturally, Chloe had been awed by the suave, handsome young lawyer. The first time she'd met him, Brice Palmer, with her father's backing, had been going for an unexpectedly vacated seat in the state senate. He'd lost, as her father had anticipated he would, but his name had become known in the right circles.

Even at their wedding, he'd been campaigning; and the next time around, he had won. As the youngest and by far the handsomest state senator, he had been a media event right from the first.

And as his bride, Chloe had found herself taken over by a cadre of experts. Thanks in large part to a father who had in turn intimidated, indulged and ignored her, she had been putty in the hands of her husband and the political advisers who groomed him on everything from the correct tie to wear to which affair, to the proper degree of warmth to allow in his camera-perfect smiles.

"Lucky devil," she'd heard one journalist remark to another. "With Baskin's money behind him and the daughter thrown in for good measure, he can't miss.

She's the perfect accessory for the well-groomed young politician.''

"Yeah. Good thing he got rid of that little red-headed cracker he was mixed up with a while back. She was ba-aad news.''

Disillusioned, but lacking the courage to break away, Chloe had gone on to become just that—the perfect accessory. She had known how to run a house such as the one her father maintained, which was fortunate, because none of his wives had ever shown much interest in anything besides spending his money. She had been taught from childhood to be gracious and charming, even when she felt like screaming and throwing things.

But even before the brief honeymoon was over, she had begun to suspect that her marriage was lacking some vital element. She had tried to talk about it to Brice.

"Not now, Chloe—we'll talk about whatever it is once I get a few minutes to spare, I promise you,'' he had told her the first few times she had broached the subject of their relationship.

After a while, it had turned into "Oh, for heaven's sake, Chloe, what do you want from me? I married you, didn't I? That proves something, doesn't it?''

Perhaps it had. But she'd never known just what. There was always another late-night session, another speech, another public-appearance tour, during which she would stand at his side in a costume chosen for her by one of his coaches, and speak lines written for her by another. She was told to dress less expensively, more modestly, less flamboyantly, more colorfully—

she was made up for television and told that her teeth absolutely *must* be capped.

Frantic over her failing marriage, she had let them dress her as if she were a doll, although she drew the line at having her perfectly good teeth meddled with.

"Brice, couldn't we have dinner together tonight, just the two of us?" she'd pleaded again and again. "We do need to talk."

But there had never been time to talk, never time for just the two of them. Even when the senate wasn't in session, there'd been so many out-of-town trips to be made—"fact-finding trips," according to Brice. Trips that had not included her.

"I have certain duties, dammit! What do you think the public elected me for—to play hanky-panky with an immature wife? Go do something for mankind, will you? Visit your old man. Make life miserable for his latest bimbo—I need a breather."

She had visited her father. She had visited an old school friend in Tampa. She had visited her cousin Ginny, who had been living in Gainesville at the time. She had shopped and redecorated her father's home and spent hours in the library, pretending to read.

She had cut ribbons, accompanied her husband to social and political functions when he considered it politically advantageous to have her along, smiling on cue and doing her best to be the "perfect accessory."

And all that time, she had never once suspected. If her father had, he'd never told her. And she had never had the courage to push herself in where she obviously wasn't wanted and find out for herself.

She used to think that if she could have had a baby...

But it was highly unlikely. Brice had known that when he married her, for she'd never made any secret of it.

Restlessly Chloe turned over and reached for the old-fashioned alarm clock on the bedside table. One-twenty. What would it take to make her sleep? She'd gone for forty-eight hours on two hours' sleep. Her eyes refused to stay open, but her mind refused to shut down.

The princess suspected that she'd been drugged. With all her will she fought against it, knowing that if she once succumbed to sleep, she would be in their evil hands, and that nothing could save her.

It was the Ukrainian spy, of course. She had suspected him the first time she'd seen him running toward her, his dark, lightly silvered hair blowing in the wind, his eyes narrowed against the late-day glare.

She had known that she would be powerless against his spell, for she was too weary to fight any longer. Too weary to run. And Mr. Y was far too compelling....

Quint stood in the doorway and stared at the slight lump under the white blanket. For a long time he watched, wondering why he hadn't simply delivered her to the emergency room and left. Wondering who she was, why she hid herself behind such impenetrable walls, and what she was doing in this neck of the woods.

Wondering why the devil he was standing here wondering, when he was practically dead on his feet.

* * *

It was still early when Chloe awoke. Could that really have been a rooster she heard? Was this a farm? Chickens inhabited farms, and male chickens were noted for rising with the sun—or so she'd always heard. She had once asked for a chicken for Easter and been told that zoning regulations forbade it.

She rather thought it had been her father's housekeeper who forbade it, just as she had forbidden kittens and puppies and anything else that might disturb the expensive tranquillity of her domain.

Shivering in the chilly morning air, Chloe listened at the door and, hearing no sound, dashed across to the bathroom, where she came face-to-face with disaster.

"Great Scott," she whispered in awe. She had seen hurricanes do less damage. Nevertheless she set about picking up the damp towels and rumpled clothing, blotting up water beside the tub, replacing caps on bottles and tubes, and straightening the shaving gear that had been used and left scattered across the lavatory surround.

Either the man had a long-suffering housekeeper who was well paid to clean up after him, or he was totally undomesticated. Or both.

Obscurely pleased to discover that Mr. Y could lay claim to at least one very human fault, Chloe ran herself a tub of hot water and settled in to soak away the assorted aches and stiffnesses that were beginning to make themselves felt.

It was almost forty minutes later when she went downstairs. The smell of burnt coffee led her to the kitchen, where she found Quinton seated at a table that was littered with used dishes, newspapers and the contents of a battered briefcase that was currently lying on its side, draped with a handsome, if slightly wrinkled, Paisley necktie.

He stared at her for a moment, blinked, and then almost tripped getting to his feet. "I didn't realize you were awake, or I would have— That is, are you feeling all right? Here—you'd better sit down."

He swept a jacket and two books off a chair and swung it closer to where she was standing. As if she cared to sit in the middle of the kitchen, three feet away from the table.

Standing there in a white flannel skirt and pale blue cotton sweater, which she suddenly realized were all wrong for this place, this season, Chloe made an effort to pull herself together.

"Good morning," she said, sounding more breathless than she had in at least fifteen years. What on earth ailed her? Granted, she was running, but hardly the four-minute mile. And definitely not on foot.

"Uh, yeah—that is, good morning," Quint replied. He felt like a ham-handed ox, standing there waiting for her to take her seat. But he couldn't very well sit down until she did.

Light from the window struck her gray-green eyes at an angle, making them appear to be lit from within. Distracted, he reminded himself of his manners and nodded again to the chair. "Please—have a seat. I'll have your breakfast ready in a minute. You can get started on coffee and—oh yeah, you like juice? There's orange or tomato, and the tomato's homemade."

"No coffee, thanks—and no breakfast. But I would like a glass of tomato juice, and if you don't mind, an aspirin?"

He bumped against his own chair, catching it before it could fall, and sent her an apologetic look. "Aspirin. Sure, you just wait right here. Sit down— Here, you might want to glance at the morning paper." He shoved it into her hands and stepped back, his hands held out as if to assure himself that she wouldn't move an inch until he got back.

Chloe laid the paper aside and smiled, shaking her head—which was beginning to ache quite badly, as were her right shoulder and her neck. If Mr. Y was the best the Ukrainians could field in the way of a secret agent, then there was little hope for them. They'd have to get along without their coveted soybean fertilizer formula.

Wishing she dared try a cup of his coffee again, she glanced around her. From the looks of his kitchen— and his bath—Quinton Stevens was either helpless as a baby or bone lazy, and somehow, he didn't strike her as either.

Clumsy, though, in a nice sort of way. He acted as if he couldn't do enough for her. That gave her a rare and comforting feeling, and Chloe decided she quite liked it. In fact, she almost regretted that she'd be leaving in an hour or so, or as soon as the garage could unbend whatever needed unbending and fix whatever there was that was broken. Quinton himself had said he didn't think there was anything seriously wrong, other than a crumpled hood and a ruined fender. How long would it take to remove them and replace them with new ones? Her father had had a fender, a windshield and a front bumper replaced on the Jaguar his latest wife had driven in less time than it had taken Bebe to explain why it wasn't her fault.

But of course, this wasn't exactly Hobe Sound. Or even Tallahassee.

"About my car," she began while Quinton rummaged in a drawer and came up with a bottle of aspirin.

"Oh, yeah—I meant to tell you. I called the garage. Buster says he can probably get it done by the middle of next week, if he gets lucky."

Chapter Three

Before the day was over, Chloe had learned three things. First of all, there was no chance that her car would be ready as soon as she had hoped. Williamston was the nearest town, and the garage there did not happen to cater to Mercedes owners. Buster had ordered the needed parts, and he hoped to have them in hand by the end of the week, when work could begin.

Second, her host, for all that he was a busy man, was the kindest, gentlest, most considerate person she could have had the good fortune to be rescued by. He didn't know her from Adam—she was almost certain of that—yet he went out of his way to make her feel welcome in his home.

Third, there was his home itself. It was a comfortable, roomy, solidly built ... pigsty!

Not that Quinton Stevens was a slob—not personally, at least. It was just, as he explained to her, that his housekeeper had retired and he had been unable to find a replacement willing to come so far out into the country. The poor woman had worked for his family for more than forty years. After both his parents died, she had stayed on to look after him, but when she wanted to go and live with her newly widowed sister, Quint hadn't the heart to keep her on.

"I'll try to locate someone to come in while you're here," he said apologetically. "Truth is, I hadn't realized how bad things had got until I saw—that is, until you..." He shrugged and smiled a crooked smile that lifted his mustache beguilingly on one side.

Chloe thought he had the kindest face she had ever seen. On the heels of that thought came another, more troubling one. He had the kind of shoulders a woman could lean on—the kind of arms that could wrap a woman in security whenever she felt needy.

And lord knows, she felt needy! At a time in her life when she could least afford to give in to weakness, all she wanted to do was curl up on his dusty, cluttered hearth and rest.

All right, Chloe Hathaway Baskin Palmer, get your brain back on-line! The last thing you need in your life is another man, and even if you were stupid enough to be interested, this one is spoken for.

His fiancée was a lucky woman. Chloe only hoped she was good enough for him. "What about your— um, that is, doesn't the woman you're engaged to know of anyone who could help out?"

He laughed then—a deep, soft chuckle that made her want to laugh right along with him. And Chloe hadn't laughed in so long, the feeling was almost frightening.

"Who, Janet? The place could fall down around her ears, and she probably wouldn't notice. She's a whiz at business, though. Got a mind like a razor. You'll like her," he went on to say, and somehow, Chloe knew right then that she wasn't going to like this paragon quite as much as she should.

Actually, she did. Janet came out to the house that first day—to look over her fiancé's unexpected houseguest, Chloe rather thought, although there was no hint of either jealousy or suspicion in her manner.

"So you're the stray," the dark-haired woman said cheerfully, extending a small, square hand in a firm handshake. "Quint was always dragging some poor homeless wretch home with him. Dogs, cats, baby possums—anything that needed feeding or patching up. His mama used to swear he deliberately held the screen door open to let the flies get to the sugar bowl."

Chloe could have chosen to be insulted. Instead, she took Janet's words at face value. Quint was a kindhearted man who had always had a soft spot for anyone weaker than he was—which included just about everyone.

"Lucky for me he saw what happened and came back to help out," she responded.

"Lucky for you he didn't go chasing off into the woods to see if the buck was all right," Janet retorted dryly. "Not that he doesn't like venison as much as the next fellow, but old Quint manages to convince himself that the deer volunteers for the mission."

Chloe smiled; Janet laughed aloud. She had a deep-bodied laugh that went along with her firm handclasp. She was open and aboveboard, and those were qualities that Chloe had good reason to value.

All the same, a bit of artifice in the way of lipstick and eye shadow would have done wonders for her looks. Her hair was unabashedly threaded with gray, and worn in a short cut that did nothing to soften her blunt features. In an oatmeal tweed suit and oxford-weave shirt, she was not a particularly feminine person, yet Chloe found her attractive for all that. And thoroughly likable.

"Hey, you've been doing things in here," Quinton accused, coming in through the door with his arms full of grocery bags just then. "I thought I told you to take it easy today."

"After sleeping all morning, I had to find something to do. I'm not used to being idle."

"What kind of work do you do?" Janet asked, and Chloe felt a wash of embarrassment.

How could she tell this quick-minded, successful businesswoman that she spoke adequate French, played adequate piano, arranged flowers like a pro, and could manage a sit-down dinner for thirty on two days' notice. Hardly a basis for a career.

"I'll check out the kitchen," Quint put in. "We brought steaks and green stuff for salad. You ladies wait here until I give the all clear, will you?"

Unconsciously assuming the role of hostess, Chloe indicated a chair and waited until Janet was seated before taking her own place. On the verge of introducing a safe topic of conversation, she suddenly realized that she was the guest here, not the other way around. But if Janet noticed anything amiss, she was kind enough to ignore it.

Before either of them could come up with an opening remark, Quint poked his head around the door, a scowl on his dark face, and commented, "I thought you said you slept all morning!"

"Are you speaking to me?" Chloe's hand fluttered protectively over her chest. "I assure you, I—"

"This place is slick as a whistle—not a dirty dish in sight!"

"Oh, but I assure you, I only—"

"And you cleaned up all the papers and dusted in the living room, and hung up my clothes, and—"

"The papers are bundled up in the storage room off the kitchen. I wasn't sure if you recycled or not—or if perhaps you hadn't got around to reading them yet. I only tidied up a bit. I had nothing better to do."

Janet's bark of laughter came as a shock. "Ha! She got you good, didn't she, Quint? Maybe you ought to see if you can hire her on as a housekeeper." She turned to Chloe, her cheeks creased in a broad grin. "D'he tell you his housekeeper quit on him? Couldn't hack it any longer. The guy's a walking disaster area—believe me, I know! You ought to see his office!"

To Chloe's astonishment, Quint actually looked embarrassed. "Oh, I'm sure it's not all that bad," she remarked in an effort to ease his discomfort.

"Not bad! Huh, you never met his mother! Camilla Stevens made a career of spoiling her menfolk, husband and son alike. Waited on 'em hand and foot, picked up after 'em like they were paralyzed or something. She'd have bled for them when they got cut if she could've figured out how to do it." Janet shook her head. "One thing we settled right up front—I'll run Quint's business for him, but damned if I'm going to waste my time mucking around the house. Either he

gets a cook and a housekeeper, or he gets himself another wife.''

She grinned as if she were waiting to be congratulated, and Chloe searched her brain for a diplomatic
response. Actually, she was rather shocked to hear
such an outburst before the wedding—usually it came
afterward, if at all.

''In that case,'' she said tentatively, ''shall I make
the salad?''

''Better you than me,'' Janet quipped. ''Whew!
After the day I had, I'm going to pour myself a bourbon and put my feet up. Call me when it's ready,
okay?''

Chloe found herself watching Quinton as he went
about laying out the steaks and readying the indoor
grill. Was it possible to feel sorry for a big, good-
looking, obviously successful man one hardly knew?

It was. And she did. No matter how hopeless he was
at keeping house, he deserved someone better than
Janet Bond. Oh, she was nice enough—friendly,
guileless, and probably brilliant at what she did. But
what sort of wife would she make?

Quinton needed a woman who...

Quinton was old enough to know precisely what he
needed. He had chosen Janet, so she must suit him.
Besides, Chloe told herself firmly, it was none of her
business. She'd be out of here before another day
passed, if she had to rent a bench at the bus station.

If there even *was* a bus station in this forsaken place.

The two of them worked quietly together, Quint
trimming the three T-bones and Chloe washing the
assorted greens and peeling tomatoes. She knew how
to cook, even though she'd done little enough of it.

Her father had insisted that she know how to do anything she asked the house servants to do, and she'd been glad of that after she'd married. Many a night she had dined alone on a homemade feast for one.

"Onions?" she asked.

"Sure. On mine, that is—Janet can't handle them. They give her heartburn."

How romantic. It was a good thing Mr. Y was a successful secret agent, because he'd never make it as a romantic hero. "Shall I make it in three separate bowls then, instead of tossing it all together?"

He beamed at her across the grill, and something that had been frozen inside Chloe for a long, long time, began to thaw. "Hey, that's a great idea! Bowls are up there—I think we have some wooden salad bowls—I usually just use a soup bowl."

There were wooden salad bowls and tarnished silver hollowware, delicate china and dime-store earthenware, all mixed in together. Neat by nature, Chloe itched to empty out the cupboard, reline it and set it to rights again.

"Could you advise me on a motel or hotel near the garage? I want to be available as soon as my car is ready." If there was one thing she knew, it was *not* to dig in and make herself at home.

The steaks hissed loudly, sending up a cloud of smoke. "Hey—you reckon I turned it up too high? I'm not the world's greatest cook, I'm afraid."

Chloe slipped around to the front of the grill. It was similar to one in her father's mountain cabin. "No, it's fine—the smoke's clearing already. You might want to switch on the exhaust, though."

She could have laughed at the look of concern on his face. What she really felt like doing was hugging the big lummox. How could any man be so capable and so helpless at the same time?

The steaks were done to perfection, thanks largely to Chloe's subtle directions. Left to Quint, her own, which she preferred well-done, would have been shoe leather.

The salads were tossed with her own oil, cheese and vinegar dressing, as the bottled ones in the refrigerator had turned rancid. In fact, the whole refrigerator looked as if it could do with a turning out.

"When did you say your housekeeper retired?" she asked as she quickly rinsed three wineglasses and dried them on a paper towel.

"Um...how long has it been, Jan? About a month?"

"More like three," Janet replied dryly.

"Yeah. I reckon I should put another ad in the paper."

"Do, and the day you sign a housekeeper to a year's contract, we'll set the date, okay?" Janet grinned. Quint's smile was a bit slower in coming, and Chloe found herself feeling sorry for both of them, for some obscure reason. Lord knows, she was no romantic, herself, but all the same...

Using the excuse of a headache, which was not all that far from the truth, Chloe retired early. The house was large, and her bedroom was at the very back. Hopefully she wouldn't be disturbed by the sound of voices from the living room.

Yet, later on, lying in bed, she found herself listening intently, perversely hoping to hear...at least something. Laughter. The clink of glasses. The sound of a closing door. Wondering, when she didn't, if they were doing something inherently quieter. Somehow she found it impossible to picture brash, matter-of-fact Janet Bond in the throes of a passionate embrace.

Strangely enough, she had no trouble at all envisioning Quint's eyelids growing heavy with desire, his firm lower lip softening as he leaned over the woman in his arms and drew her tightly against the swell of his hard chest....

Muttering a mild oath, Chloe rolled over in bed and then grabbed the sore place at the back of her head. If she didn't know better, she'd have thought she'd struck it in the accident. It was becoming decidedly painful in that one area just to the left of center....

But there was no possible way she could have struck the back of her head. It was probably just another headache—Lord knows, she'd had enough of those over the past few years. This one was in a different place than usual, that was all.

According to her alarm clock, it was just after midnight when Chloe gave up and went in search of some aspirin. Unsure whether or not Quint and Janet were still downstairs, she tiptoed to the upstairs bathroom. There, among the shaving gear, the scissors and bandages and such, she located an empty aspirin bottle. "Oh, drat," she muttered, wondering if an ice pack would help. She would never get to sleep at this rate. If only—

The kitchen. That was where Quint had found the aspirins for her before. She only hoped he hadn't given her the last two in the bottle. Before she left, she would make him a shopping list, heading it with aspirin and adding all the other things that she'd noticed he needed. Such as dishwashing detergent. And paper towels. And salad dressing. Silently, she added to the list as she crept down the stairs. At the foot of the landing, she risked a peep into the living room.

It was illuminated only by the light from the hallway. So she'd been right—they were in there making out. Or making love. Or whatever a man did with a woman like Janet.

Oh, Lord, she was feeling bitchy. Janet was a perfectly nice woman—attractive in an understated way, and smart as a whip. Hadn't she kept them entertained all through dinner with a rundown on every commercial building project in a two-county area—the demographics, the contractors, the backers, the prime tenants and the built-in risk factors?

"Aspirin," she muttered. Where had he gotten them from? Over the sink? Beside the refrigerator? "If I were a bottle of aspirins, where would I—?"

"Chloe? What's the matter? Couldn't you sleep?"

She dropped the bottle she'd just closed her fingers around, and watched in horror as it splintered on the porcelain drainboard. And then, to her everlasting shame, she burst into tears.

Quint was beside her in an instant. "Whoa, now, honey. It's not that bad. Tell me about it, hmm?"

Muffled in his arms, her face pressed against his rumpled shirt, Chloe drew in a shaky breath and tried to regain her composure. It wasn't at all like her to fall apart. She *never* cried. And Lord knows, she'd had reason enough to cry.

"I'm s-sorry," she blubbered, trying to push herself away. "It's nothing, really—nothing at all."

He wasn't buying it. "Okay, so it was the steak. I warned you not to overcook it, but would you listen? Oh, no, you had to go and incinerate a perfectly good cut of beef, and now—"

Chloe gave a small, ragged laugh, sniffed, and dragged her arm across her drenched eyes. "The steak was p-perfect, it was the—the coffee."

"Too weak?" His arms were like a steel cradle, holding her gently, but making it impossible for her to escape.

"Too weak to stand alone, maybe, but with a little help..."

This time her laughter was stronger, and he joined in. She could hear the marvelous sound deep inside his chest, and it brought a rash of goose bumps to the surface of her arms.

"You're cold. Honey, why didn't you sing out if you needed something. Was it aspirin? Does your head hurt?"

She nodded, and then wished she hadn't. "I didn't want to bother you and Janet."

"She's already gone home. Look, let me get you back in bed, and I'll bring you up a dose. I keep a first-aid kit in my car—won't take a minute to fetch it inside."

"Thank you," she said, her composure once more intact except for the occasional shuddering sob. She *hated* any sign of weakness in herself. That was the very last thing she could afford. "I'll wait here in the kitchen."

"You'll do no such thing," Quint corrected. Before she realized what he was about, he had swept her up in his arms and was headed for the stairs.

"Please put me down—this is absurd," she whispered fiercely.

He ignored her. She struggled briefly and then surrendered, bearing the indignity with all the good grace she could muster. She'd had the foresight to put on her negligee instead of coming down in just her gown, but she hadn't bothered to dig out her slippers.

"There, that's a good girl—I'd hate like the devil to drop you on your back bumper. Wouldn't do your headache much good, would it?"

She sniffed disdainfully, only to discover that he smelled good. Like wool and laundry detergent and musk, with a faint hint of bourbon and after-shave. Like a healthy, virile male.

Shouldering open her door, he lowered her onto the bed and stood back, gazing down at her with a lazy grin that revealed a row of even white teeth under his dark brown mustache.

Quint was having considerable trouble with his breathing, and he didn't think it was because he was out of shape. She wasn't all that heavy, despite her height.

Dammit, he wished she wouldn't wear that perfume around him! Janet smelled like soap and tobacco, and he could handle that just fine; but the subtle, teasing fragrance that drifted up from Chloe's clean, shiny hair was having a peculiar effect on his metabolism. Not to mention the effect of her fragile, feminine body in those few ounces of pale gray silk.

"Better let me dust off your feet," Quint said, kneeling beside the bed. And before she could stop him, he'd lifted both her bare feet in one of his large hands and was brushing off the soles. "My floors aren't what you might call real sanitary. Reckon I've sort of let things slide lately."

With tremors running from her instep all the way to her navel, it was all Chloe could do to breathe. Speech was out of the question. She stared up at the benign giant with the crinkled eyes and the warm smile and wondered if she had stepped through a looking glass somewhere along the way.

Surely this wasn't Chloe Baskin Palmer, daughter of the late Hathaway Harrington Baskin III—wife of the late senator Wilfred Brice Pickel Palmer. The well-bred Mrs. Baskin Palmer would never in this world allow herself to be found in a strange bed in a strange house, having her feet caressed by a strange man.

"Back in a jiffy," Quint told her, lowering her feet slowly to the bed and pulling up the thick layer of covers. He backed out, beaming at her as if she were a big chocolate bunny he'd found in his Easter basket.

Bemused, Chloe listened to the sound of his feet galloping down the staircase and prayed he wouldn't trip and fall before he reached the bottom. He was no Fred Astaire. Hadn't he blundered smack into the kitchen table when she'd held out a forkful of salad and asked him to come and taste her dressing?

Oh, Lord, she was finally falling apart. The back of her head was splitting, she had a bruise the size of an eggplant on her right forearm and a belt burn on her left shoulder that came all the way down over her breast. And in spite of all that, she couldn't keep her mind off a man she'd known less than thirty-six hours—a man who was newly engaged!

Could she have left the real Chloe Baskin Palmer somewhere between Florida and North Carolina? And if she had, was it really any great loss?

Reaching behind her, she drew the pins out of her coil of hair and let it tumble onto her shoulders while she waited for Quint to return with her dose of aspirin. If she had any brains at all, she would have asked him to leave it in the bathroom and let her get it herself—although trying to deflect a man like Quint Stevens from his chosen course would be like trying to turn away a column of armored tanks.

She heard the front door slam, the sound of a car door, and then the front door slammed again. Each time she winced. He was precisely the type of man she had been brought up to despise. He lived in a hovel, and if he possessed a single social grace, it was nowhere in evidence.

So why did she feel this extraordinary urge to curl up in his arms and shut out the rest of the world? To forget scandal sheets and the microphones shoved under her nose whenever she ventured outside, and the rude questions shouted at her from the mobs of reporters that had clustered outside her home, outside the courtroom and later, outside her father's home?

Because she wasn't herself. That was the only possible excuse. She would take her medicine and pray she could get to sleep before morning. And then, she would make herself some tea and toast and settle down with the phone book.

There had to be *some* place she could stay that was within walking distance of the garage. For reasons that defied understanding, she was beginning to get a bit too involved here, and that was the one thing she could not afford to do.

If worse came to worst, she would call Ginny and borrow enough money to get to Keedysville. But first she had to get a Maryland map and find out just where the place was.

Chapter Four

Chloe would have given five hundred dollars for thirty minutes with a masseuse. Or ten minutes in a whirlpool or a sauna. It took every bit of willpower she could muster to force herself to climb out of bed at half past nine.

It was obvious that Quinton had made an effort to tidy the bathroom before he had left, but the wet towel he had flung across the shower rod had slid off onto the floor, and in jamming a fresh bath set on the towel shelf, he had upset a box of talcum powder on the shelf above.

Swearing gently, she bent to pick up the damp towel, every muscle in her body protesting. He had tried. She would give him credit for that. His shaving gear had been ruthlessly raked to one side, leaving her room for her own toiletries.

She stared at her image in the mirror, not at all surprised to see the dark shadows under her eyes. On some women, shadowy eyes looked romantic. On her, with her hollow cheeks and the remnants of her 15 SPF suntan, they looked ghastly.

Unfortunately, she felt no better than she looked.

While she showered, moisturized, brushed and dressed, Chloe began compiling a mental list, the first priority being to find herself an inexpensive, convenient motel. Quint had been kindness itself, but he hadn't taken her in to raise her. The least she could do to repay him was to avoid taking advantage of his hospitality any more than she already had.

As for the hospital bill, she would just have to wait awhile longer. She hadn't gotten around to shopping for medical insurance after Brice's death, having just begun to cope with the details of everyday living again when her father—

The phone rang, and she froze, lipstick in hand, while she wondered whether or not to answer it. After the seventh shrill summons, she gave in.

"This is the Stevens residence," she said cautiously.

Quinton greeted her cheerfully. "Good morning. How're you feeling? I figured I'd better let you sleep as long as you could. Did I wake you?"

"Not at all. I've been awake for some time now."

"Good! Look, Mrs. Palmer—that is, may I call you Chloe?" Neither of them mentioned the fact that he already did. "Chloe, I left the keys to my car on the hall table in a bowl. You're welcome to use it if you need to go anywhere, but don't worry about food. I'll stop by the barbecue place and bring home lunch, okay? You want french fries with your sandwich? Or would you rather have a barbecue plate?''

"Oh, please, I—''

"Great. Chopped or sliced? This place trims it real lean, so they're both good.''

"Mr. Stevens, I think—''

"Quint.''

"I beg your pardon?''

"Quinton. It's my name, but most folks call me Quint.''

"Yes, well...as I was saying, I'll be looking for some place to stay until my car is finished, so it really isn't necessary for you to bother with—''

In spite of the deep drawl, there was an unmistakable steeliness in his tone when he interrupted her. "I seldom bother with anything I don't feel like bothering with. The gas tank's only about a quarter full. Stop by Gilmour's, on the left just before you get into town, and tell 'im to fill it up for you and put it on my account.''

She was silent for so long that he said, "Chloe? You still there?''

"How can you do this?'' she asked faintly.

"How can I do what?'' And then— "Look, I've got another call coming in. Can we talk about whatever it is that's bugging you over lunch? See you about twelve-thirty. Some iced tea would be nice, but you don't have to bother if you don't want to. I can use instant.''

She was still holding the phone, staring numbly at a faded reproduction of a square-rigger on a moonlit sea, when he said, "Chloe—the aspirin's in the bathroom. I've got a heating pad if you need it, and there's a cold pack in the freezer. Why don't you just go back to bed, huh? I'll wake you when I get home.''

It sounded heavenly, only Chloe knew she would never sleep. Her mind kept spinning like a hamster on a treadmill. If she didn't do *something*, she might fly apart.

She would start with a cup of coffee. Caffeine was the last thing her body needed, but if she went too long without it, her headache would be even worse than it was.

Besides, she felt drawn to Quint's old-fashioned, untidy kitchen. Her father's new Cuban chef had jealously guarded his territory, and she had always been slightly intimidated by the surgical white-tile-and-stainless-steel atmosphere of the kitchen in Brice's house.

Funny—she had never thought of it as their house, much less hers. In the five years of her marriage, she could count on her fingers the number of dinners she had prepared for the two of them. Brice, even when he was in town, had preferred to dine out.

"Enough!" she muttered, pouring herself a cup of Quint's caustic coffee. It was an eye-opener, she would say that much for it. With enough cream and sugar, it was even fairly palatable.

After wiping up a trail of cereal crumbs and a dribble of spilled milk on the counter, she made herself a slice of toast and nibbled on it while she brewed a pitcher of strong tea.

Then she rinsed the pan, the strainer and her own cup, and glanced around, checking to make sure that everything was in order.

Order. If there was one thing she was in desperate need of, it was a sense of order—a feeling that her world was not going to turn upside down and come crashing in on her the moment she closed her eyes. Quinton Stevens's home might not be the most orderly place she had ever seen, but it offered her the one thing that was worth more to her just now than any number of expensive, flawlessly decorated, immaculately kept houses.

It offered her privacy. And privacy would buy her time. Time to heal, time to forget—and time to plan.

The barbecue was delicate and subtly seasoned, and before she quite realized it, Chloe found herself picking up the last shreds with her fingers and licking them off.

They ate in the kitchen, and she decided then and there that if she was ever again in the position to own a house, it was going to have a warm, welcoming kitchen with a large wooden table centered by a blue granite-ware bowl of speckled homegrown pears.

"Would you care for another glass of tea?"

Quint held out his glass. "What's the secret to making this stuff? No matter how long I boil it, it never tastes right."

She couldn't repress a peal of laughter, but on seeing the spark of dawning interest in his eyes, she turned away to get more ice before refilling his glass. "It's really very simple. I'll show you how before I leave." Taking her seat again, she carefully folded her paper napkin and laid it across her plastic plate.

"There's plenty of time yet." Quint drained his third glass of iced tea. "This is almost as good as the tea my mama used to make."

Chloe found herself smiling again. The man had a curious effect on her—one she might have enjoyed exploring under different circumstances. "Janet was right," she teased gently. "You have been spoiled, haven't you?"

"I wouldn't exactly call it that."

"No? What would you call it?"

He shrugged, and Chloe watched as he blotted a glistening drop of moisture from his thick mustache. It occurred to her that she had never before known a man with a mustache—not intimately, at least.

Nor did she know this one intimately, she reminded herself, feeling her face grow warm at the very idea.

"Quint, do you know of a decent motel within walking distance of the garage where my car's been taken?" she asked for the third time.

He raked his chair back from the table, slung one ankle across his knee and studied her for several moments before replying. "Tell me something—if there was one, could you really afford it?"

She stiffened and an indignant retort formed on the tip of her tongue, when he went on to say, "I checked out your purse, remember? So I know exactly how—"

"You had no right to do that!"

"—how much cash you have on you. I know you don't carry plastic, and unless you've got a letter of credit stashed away in that classy luggage of yours, you're going to have trouble getting your car out of hock, much less paying room and board in a motel."

Quint hated himself for pushing her to the wall, especially when he saw the way the color fled from under her light golden tan. Normally he was a pretty easygoing guy, but for some reason this woman got to him, made him act dangerously out of character.

"You have no knowledge whatsoever of my financial position."

"Maybe—maybe not. I know you wear expensive clothes that are a couple of sizes too big. I know you drive a late-model 380SL that's currently running up a pretty hefty tab at Buster's Garage and Towing Service. Aside from that—"

"I assure you, I can well afford to pay for having my car repaired."

He could feel her defenses click into place. The woman had more security walls than the state pen. "Yeah, sure—the same way you could afford to pay the tab at the hospital, right?"

Before he even heard the air leave her lungs, he was wishing he could recall the words. "Look, this is crazy. We both know you need a place to stay, and we both know I've got space enough for you and your whole damned family here. So what's the problem? Stay until your car's ready—or at least until you're back on your feet again. Then you can do whatever you want to do—no strings, no questions. All right?"

It occurred to him that if her spine got any stiffer, it was going to lock in place. The more he was with her, the more he realized that the air of brittleness she wore like a suit of armor had little or nothing to do with the accident. She had the look of someone who'd been walking a tightrope over the jaws of hell.

And he wasn't helping matters a damned bit. "Hey, look—I'm sorry. I had no right to say all that stuff."

"Oh? Which *stuff* was that?" she asked coolly. The glimmer of humor that flickered briefly in her eyes made him oddly hungry for another of her rare smiles.

"The Orientals have this philosophy—you save a life, you're responsible for it. I didn't exactly save yours, but—"

"No, you didn't. As a matter of fact, if you hadn't distracted me, I never would have hit that tree in the first place."

His eyebrows peaked in surprise. "Distracted you! Lady, you *must* have hit your head!"

Was it his imagination, or was she actually turning pink again? Leaning forward, Quint forced her to look at him. "Chloe? Mind telling me how I distracted you? I don't own a bumper sticker, and my license plate can't be all that interesting."

Ducking her head again, she smoothed her pleated white sharkskin slacks over her thighs. "I didn't exactly mean 'distracted'—at least not deliberately."

In spite of his recent resolution to ease up on her, Quint couldn't let it pass. Mrs. High-and-Mighty-from-Florida was as antsy as a fourteen-year-old girl on her first date. And for reasons he didn't care to go into, Quint was finding himself more and more intrigued. "Chloe? Look at me, won't you? What exactly did you mean, then?"

She lifted her face, her elegant features at odds with her obvious embarrassment. "If you must know, my mind wandered, that's all! You happened to be the only other car on the highway, and on occasions—

when I drive by myself, that is—at least on long trips . . ."

"When you drive by yourself," he prompted when she seemed unable or unwilling to go on.

"I was playing a road game with myself! For goodness' sake," she snapped, "don't you ever play road games?"

Slowly, he shook his head, and she lifted her too-thin shoulders and let them fall in defeat.

"Forget it. My mind wandered, that's all. I'd been driving for too long, and—"

"Not trying to make it up from Florida in one stretch, were you?"

"No, of course not. I do have more sense than that."

He grinned again, and wondered what it would take to get under that polished surface of hers. And just what he would find if he did.

"Excuse me," she muttered, and left him staring after her, his dark eyes alive with curiosity—and something more.

If Chloe had not been depressed before, the call from the garage would have done the trick. She sat in an enormous brown leather wing chair and stared unseeingly at the cold fireplace. Quint had offered to build a fire, even though it wasn't terribly cold outside. She'd told him not to bother on her account, and he hadn't.

Well, at least she knew the worst now. Getting her car out of hock was going to cost roughly four thousand dollars more than she had. And that was only the estimate. How many times in the past few years had she thought things couldn't get any worse?

How many times had she been proved wrong?

Even before her marriage, Chloe had been aware of a vague emptiness, in spite of her busy social life. Her father's social life, to be more precise, for even during his brief forays into remarriage, she'd been too busy catering to his wishes to cultivate her own set of friends.

She had thought marriage would change all that, but it hadn't. She had merely exchanged one ruthlessly driven male for another. Long before Brice's private plane had crashed off Bimini with no survivors, she had stopped loving him. If, indeed, she ever had.

Even so, she'd been totally unprepared for the redheaded woman from Georgia who claimed to have been Brice's common-law wife. And as if that weren't enough of a shock, the woman had produced a son bearing Brice's name—a small image of his father, who had evidently been conceived either shortly before or shortly after Chloe's marriage to Brice.

After the first few days of opening her front door only to have a battery of flashbulbs go off in her face and a cluster of microphones shoved at her mouth, Chloe had decided not to fight. If the child were really Brice's, then whatever Brice had left belonged to him.

Chloe would have granted him that, willingly enough, but the woman had never given her the opportunity. Instead, she had come armed with lawyers and newspaper reporters, so there was no keeping anything quiet.

All Chloe had wanted was to be left alone; and to that end she had finally escaped to her father's home. He'd been between wives at the time, and much too distracted, thankfully, to bother her with more questions. Two days after she'd arrived, bag and baggage, on his doorstep, he had left for Switzerland on a business trip.

Eventually it had died down—the furor that always arose whenever a prominent social and political figure was involved in a juicy scandal. The tabloids had blown it all out of proportion, but even they had moved on to the next ten-day wonder after a while.

And then, just when she was beginning to be able to go about without dark glasses and a scarf around her head, her father had committed suicide. Four days later it had been disclosed that for years he had been systematically looting his own bank, probably to pay alimony to the three women he had been briefly married to since her mother had died when Chloe was eleven.

Once more, her world had come crashing down on her head. If the press had been bad, the lawyers and the endless creditors had been worse—they had closed in on her like a school of piranhas. She had been forced to sell everything, and even then it had not been enough. Finally, when all she had left were her clothes and her car, she had fled.

Luckily the Mercedes had been her own, bought shortly before her marriage had ended, with stock her mother had left her. She had stubbornly held on to it, even though the bank's lawyers would have liked her to sell that, too, to help repay some of her father's debts.

She'd had to prove to the courts that the car had not been a gift from her father; meanwhile, the press had had a field day reporting every excruciating detail of this latest scandal, including the rather colorful personal lives of each of her father's wives, and then embellishing the whole affair with a rehash of the Brice Palmer—Sheila Warden-Chloe Baskin affair.

She had cut her losses and run the very minute she was free. But now the expensive automobile, which she'd counted on to get her as far away as possible from all that, and then to set her up until she could support herself, was a crumpled mass of steel on the floor of some ''nowhere'' garage.

If she were a cursing woman, she would have turned the air blue, for all the good it would have done her. She'd sooner curse than cry; but the truth was, she was no good at either form of release.

After selling all her jewelry—from Brice's showy wedding and engagement rings to her grandmother's stunning emeralds—to pay off her father's domestic staff and the most urgent outstanding household bills, she had counted on the proceeds from the sale of her car to buy her a quick course in whatever seemed feasible at the time. She had no idea what the job market in Keedysville, Maryland, would be like. All she wanted was to be near family, and her cousin Ginny filled the bill.

They'd always gotten along well together, despite the differences in their natures. Ginny was a born leader, an adventurer, an independent from their kindergarten days on, while Chloe had always been at best a rather timid follower. She used to make up stories in which her hair turned black like her cousin's, and she magically took on all Ginny's courage and daring. Ginny, who had lived only three miles away in those days, had laughed and told her not to be a "noggin."

Chloe had yet to discover what a noggin was—she only knew she didn't enjoy being one.

So now what? Even if she decided to forgo all cosmetic work on the car, the cost of getting her grubstake running again would be far beyond her meager resources. Why couldn't she simply have bought herself a nice little Chevrolet sedan instead of a luxury car with two tops? At least the repairs wouldn't have been so outrageously expensive.

She would just have to see if Buster would take the car itself as payment for repairing it, and give her the balance of its value in cash.

Did buses run between Williamston and Keedysville? she wondered.

Quint called from work in the middle of the afternoon to invite her to dinner with himself and Janet. "Nothing fancy. Janet is no better at cooking than I am, so we usually eat out."

"I thought your fiancée lived with her mother."

"She does. But I don't like to impose on Jessica's hospitality too often."

Chloe could sympathize with that feeling. "I'd really rather not, if you don't mind. I'll have one of your eggs and make myself a pot of tea, if I may."

"Well, sure… You may do anything you like. I just thought you might like to get out and see something of the countryside."

Chloe took that to mean he would like her to get out. To her own irritation, she was disappointed rather than relieved, and it showed in the stiffness of her reply.

"Thank you very much, then. Perhaps afterward you could drop me off at a motel in town. I presume there is such a thing...?"

Chapter Five

I hate olives on my pizza," Janet said. "You know that, Quint."

"I like 'em. I thought maybe if Chloe did, she and I could take that part and leave you the rest."

"Are these anchovies? Good Lord, what happened to your brain today? I hope you're in better shape when we meet with Adamson about that riverfront tract of his. He's no fool, you know."

Ignoring his fiancée's irritable mood, Quint levered slices of hot pizza off the cardboard support and doled them out. He liked anchovies. He liked olives. When Janet ordered for them at work, she consistently ignored his likes and catered to her own.

"Here you go, Chloe—olives and anchovies suit you?"

Looking quickly from one to the other, Chloe nodded and reached for her plate. She was hungry enough so that not even their squabbling could dull her appetite.

As she bit into the thick, cheesy slab, she wondered, not for the first time, what had attracted these two people to each other—not that she couldn't see all too clearly what had attracted Janet. Quinton was strong, reliable, kind—the sort of man a woman could lean on when the going got rough. Add to that the fact that he positively exuded a quiet but very potent brand of sexiness, and it was no wonder the woman was smitten!

But as far as she could see, they didn't agree on much of anything. Quint didn't seem to care how disheveled his house was, as long as he was comfortable. Janet obviously adhered to the theory of a place for everything and everything in its place—as long as she wasn't the one to have to put it there.

Quint would mention a book he had particularly enjoyed, or a political appointment he disagreed with—or even a recent treasure find off the Carolina coast. Janet would stare at him abstractedly for a moment and then steer the conversation right back to business, as if he had never spoken.

Did the woman ever think about anything besides property and development?

"How is it?" Quint asked, catching her with her mouth full. "Pretty good pizza, huh?"

Chloe nodded, managing to smile at the same time, and he beamed right back at her, obviously pleased as all get-out that someone shared his taste in *something* even if it was only olives and anchovies.

Chloe's years of experience in pouring oil on troubled social waters came into play as she introduced the one subject that would interest any bride-to-be. "Have you set a date yet?"

"Set a date? I have an on-site appointment with John Adamson on the twenty-first, but— Oh. You mean to get married."

Chloe feared her expression had given her away before she could bring it under control. Could any supposedly intelligent woman really be that dense?

"I've always thought Thanksgiving was a lovely time for a wedding," Chloe murmured. Which, to put it bluntly, was a bald-faced lie. There was no such thing as a lovely time for a wedding. But then, having grown up in an atmosphere of social lies, Chloe had long since discovered their value. She felt sorry for Quint, but at the moment, she simply lacked the stamina to pretend an interest in building codes, zoning boards, perk tests or any of Janet's other favorite topics of conversation.

Quint spoke up. He had refreshed their drinks— beer for Janet, milk for Chloe and iced tea for himself. "I reckon we're sort of waiting until Janet has time to figure out what she wants to do to the house."

"The house. You mean this house?" Chloe glanced around her. They were in the kitchen, which, while hopelessly old-fashioned, was a charming and comfortable room. The dining room, she had soon discovered, served as a home office; its round oak table was piled high with papers and drafting instruments, and scattered with the crisp brown leaves of a moribund Boston fern.

"Sure," Quint replied. "You don't think I'm going to move in with Janet's mother, do you?"

Not having had the pleasure of meeting Mrs. Bond or seeing her home, Chloe had no idea whether or not he was being sarcastic. After consideration, she thought not. Quint was far too direct to resort to sarcasm.

"Live with Mama? Lord no!" Janet put in. "One of the main reasons I'm marrying Quint is so I can get away from Mama. I swear to you, it's the first time I've ever done anything to please that woman. Quint can tell you—Mama's been dead set on having one of her daughters marry a Stevens. She'd never admit it, but I think she had something going with old man J.Q., Quint's daddy, before she married Papa. Anyhow, ever since Quint and Marissa were—"

"Chloe, if you're finished, why don't we go in the living room and leave this mess until later."

Startled at the touch of steel she detected in his voice, Chloe rose and looked from one to the other. "Why don't you two go on, and I'll just whisk this stuff away and make coffee. You do trust me to make coffee, don't you, Quinton?"

"There's still some in the pot from breakfast if you want to reheat it," he suggested helpfully.

Chloe shuddered. "I'll just be a minute," she replied, already planning to serve coffee and disappear as quickly as she could. It was bad enough being a third wheel to a newly engaged couple—although Quint and Janet were far from behaving like a typical engaged couple. They didn't seem like a couple at all; but then, they were both well past the first bloom of youth. They'd probably been having an affair for years.

Marissa? Quint and Marissa? Marissa who?

Frowning, she scoured the coffeepot and set it to brew six cups. It would take three cups to equal the strength of one of Quint's usual brew.

" . . . when you have a perfectly good furnace," Janet was saying when Chloe came through the door bearing a tray.

Quint immediately leaped up to help her. "Here, you shouldn't be carrying heavy things in your condition."

Chloe's jaw dropped. Janet merely looked blank. "You're just out of the hospital," he elaborated, taking her arm to ease her down onto the sofa, after first having tossed aside Janet's coat.

"I wasn't in it, I was *at* it," Chloe corrected. "There's a big difference. Besides, I didn't need to be there in the first place."

"You've had these headaches—"

"Do you usually go to the hospital when you have a headache?"

Quint's brows pulled to meet over his thrusting nose. "If I'd just wrapped a damned car around a damned pine tree, you can bet your sweet a—"

"Knock it off, will you? If she's got a headache, the last thing she needs is you nagging at her." Janet poured herself a cup of coffee and sipped experimentally. "Not bad," she said. "A little weak, but then, I never could make a decent cup of the stuff, myself. Usually drink instant."

Quint graciously abstained from comment, but he went on watching Chloe as if expecting her to fall over in a dead faint at any moment.

Determined to prove that she was in no danger of imminent collapse, Chloe smiled brightly and looked from one to the other. "So... what were you two discussing when I came in? Furnaces? I'll have to admit, that's a subject I know nothing whatsoever about. Father was thinking of having a heat pump put in before..."

As quickly as it had come, her spurious brightness fled. Quint reached out and gently removed the cup from her hand. Seeing his look of concern, she forced herself to go on. "We Floridians have shamefully thin blood, you know. Actually, I once had a fireplace, but it was never used." Brice's sleek, freestanding white fireplace, centered in his white-carpeted, white-furnished room, with all his sleek, decorator abstracts...

She resurrected her smile. "Sooner or later, I'm going to have to go shopping for some warmer clothes. I thought I'd wait until I got to Maryland."

She'd been chattering without thinking, but the moment Quint met her eyes, she knew precisely what he was thinking. *Shopping with what? The same thing you're going to use to get your car out of hock? The same thing you used to pay your bill at the emergency room the other night?*

It was Janet who inadvertently came to her rescue. "He's got a practically new oil furnace in the basement, but he insists on using this stinky old fireplace. Did you ever see such a mess? Lord knows when's the last time it was cleaned out. I was just telling him he ought to vacuum it well and then nail a cover over it. Do you have any idea how much heat is lost up that chimney?"

Chloe hadn't a glimmer. Instead, she had a quick mental image of a roaring fire, toasting marshmallows, slippered feet—two pairs—on the hearth, and soft music somewhere in the background. She sighed, oblivious to the quiet speculation in Quint's eyes as he watched her shadowed face grow wistful in the imaginary firelight.

From fireplaces, they went on to talk of other things. It seemed that Quint's house, with its mixture of heavy, masculine pieces and ornate Victoriana, gave Janet claustrophobia.

Chloe had to agree that it was a decorator's worst nightmare. The big leather chair and ottoman, as well as the huge oak desk that crowded the spindly what-not, were Quint's additions to his mother's furnishings.

"Why not move the smaller things into the dining room and let it be an extension of your living room?" Chloe suggested.

"But then, what would we do for a dining room?" Janet questioned.

"What would I do with all my papers?" Quint asked at the same time.

Chloe didn't know. She didn't particularly care, but as long as she was at it, she might as well give them something to think about besides construction and development. "There's that enormous utility room off the kitchen...."

"Used to be the kitchen. In the old days when people cooked with wood, the kitchens were separate so that cooking didn't heat up the rest of the house," Quint told her.

"Or burn it to the ground," Janet added dryly, and Chloe shot her a smile. If she could get them both in-volved in something besides business, it would be wonderful—she might even feel as if she'd repaid Quint for his hospitality.

"Well, why not turn it into a dining room? How many times would you need a formal dining room, after all, with such a wonderful family-size kitchen?"

"You can turn it into Buckingham Palace as far as I'm concerned," Janet snapped, and she lit her fourth cigarette and exhaled a stream of smoke toward the ceiling. "Until Quint locates a housekeeper to move in and take charge of this place, I'm staying put. Mama may be a pain in the butt, but at least she's got a cook and cleaning lady."

"I put an ad in the paper yesterday," Quint said with a distinctly unloverlike look at his fiancée.

Janet snorted. There was no other word to describe it. "It'd better pay off. I didn't sweat out my M.B.A. just so I could muck around somebody's kitchen, I can tell you that."

"I believe we're all aware of your sentiments, Janet," Quint responded quietly.

"I speak my mind. Do you have a problem with that?"

Chloe wanted to disappear. How could any man sit back and take such outrageous behavior from any woman? Why would he want to?

More to the point, why should any woman agree to marry a man when she obviously had no feeling for him at all?

"And while we're on the subject of this house of yours, why don't you get rid of all this old junk your folks collected, and then we can choose something modern and practical. The dining room would hold two filing cabinets and two desks if we throw out that godawful buffet, and we could bring in the spare copier from the office.''

Poor Quint, Chloe thought. *The handsome prince married his wonderful princess and carried her off to his castle, where she immediately took charge of his army and turned against him, throwing him into the dungeon and claiming his kingdom for herself.*

"Why don't you jot down a few ideas, Chloe?" Quint suggested as she was trying to think of a graceful way to excuse herself.

"Ideas?"

"About what to do—how to make this place livable again?"

"You mean like—decorating ideas?" She glanced at Janet, expecting to see some sign of resentment. Instead of resentment, she saw relief.

"Lord, yes," Janet responded with a gusty sigh. "Better you than me! As long as you're stuck here anyway, waiting for your car to get patched up, would you mind too much? I don't have a clue about that sort of thing. Don't give much of a damn, frankly. But then, we can't all be domesticated little hausfraus, can we? Some of us were blessed—or cursed—with a functioning brain."

Stunned at such a blatant lapse in manners, Chloe couldn't help but glance at Quint. But if he'd heard, he showed no sign. Instead he was scowling at the cold fireplace, apparently deep in his own dark thoughts.

Poor Janet. Poor Quint. Chloe felt a crazy urge to giggle, and decided it was long past time she retired. She really was feeling tired. And sore. But not quite so depressed, oddly enough. Her own problems were almost over, but Quint's were only beginning.

Nor did she care to hang around and watch him suffer. For reasons she didn't care to explore, he was becoming far too important to her. She wanted better for him than Janet Bond. He deserved a wife who adored him, who would make a home for him, and talk about building houses instead of commercial development when he wanted to discuss his work, and let him feel free to talk about treasure hunting. He deserved a wife who would give him children; and somehow, she couldn't see Janet in that role.

She could picture a sturdy little boy following his father around the yard, feeding dogs, or chickens—learning about responsibility and caring and all those other wonderful qualities that made a man like Quinton Stevens so rare.

His son would have thick dark hair, so straight it flopped down over his forehead, and a pair of dark eyes that would melt the coldest heart.

"Good night, you two. And thanks for the pizza."

Janet looked blank for a moment, as if she'd forgotten that Chloe was even there. Quint smiled, his eyes crinkling at the corners in a way that made her feel weak-kneed. "Good night, Chloe. Better get out another blanket, it's supposed to drop into the thirties tonight."

A short while later, Chloe stepped under the shower and lathered herself ruthlessly with Quint's pine-scented soap. Tonight she was going to sleep. She was going to sleep eight hours, and she was *not* going to dream. And when she woke up, she was going to see about leaving this place just as soon as possible.

* * *

The pain was almost nauseating. Chloe opened one eye to see a gray, dreary rain beating against the tall window, and groaned softly.

What on earth was happening to her? This was no ordinary headache—it felt as if the back of her head were about to explode.

Aspirin... She had to take something, and quickly!

Easing her legs out from under the covers, she grabbed the bedside table to steady herself and her hand struck the alarm clock, which went skittering across the painted floor. It came to rest against the rocker and set forth an ear-penetrating sound that made her cringe.

"Oh, Lord," she moaned, feeling the back of her head for any sign of swelling. There was none, but if that clock didn't run down soon, she was going to die.

"Chloe? Are you all right?"

It was Quint. She tried to answer that she was just fine so that he would go away and let her die in peace, but the clock was screaming at her, and her head was splitting, and all she could utter was a thin little whimper.

Quint shoved the door open, but managed to catch it before it banged against the wall. He was bending over her in an instant, concern written plainly on his tough, masculine features. "Hey, now, what's the matter, honey? Come on, now. It can't be all that bad." He reached out and thumbed a tear from her cheek, and that was the first Chloe knew that she was crying.

No—not actually crying. Just no longer strong enough to hold back the tears. There was an important difference, although it escaped her at the moment.

"Something bothering you?" he asked gruffly. "Something besides a wrecked car, some nasty bruises and a flat wallet, that is?" Sitting beside her on the bed, he gathered her against his chest so that her face nestled quite naturally in the curve between his neck and his shoulder. Chloe wanted to crawl into his warmth and hide from the pain.

She tried to laugh, but it came out as a sob. "Oh, damn," she mumbled into his collar. She sniffed, and again she was acutely aware of the scent of his body— the soap-sun-wool-musk smell that was so oddly comforting. Perhaps because Brice had always smelled of cologne, Quint's contrasting lack of artifice was reassuring in the most basic way.

"My head hurts again—this time, though, it feels like a—an injury of some sort. Quint, would you please look and see what's happening?"

Holding her away from him, he took her face between his hands, and she felt as if she were drowning in the depth of his eyes. "Show me where it hurts," he rumbled softly.

"Back here—" She ducked her head so that the top rested against his chest. "Just to the left of center, down low—sort of behind my ear. I thought I felt a lump, but I'm not sure...."

She could feel his fingers searching through her hair. The pain was exquisite, yet his touch didn't seem to make it worse. She opened her eyes, and finding herself staring at his lap, she was shocked to discover herself wondering what would happen if she weren't in pain. If there were no Janet. And if Quinton—

"Can't see a blessed thing that doesn't look right. Maybe a slight swelling right here, but I'm not even sure about that," he said, and she shut her eyes quickly, embarrassed at where her thoughts had wandered for an instant. Even at the best of times, she had never been particularly...physical. And this was hardly the best of times.

Oh, God, could it be a tumor? Had it been growing all this time, until it had begun to affect her thoughts—her very personality? Her head felt as if it were about to burst open like ripe fig, and in spite of the pain—in spite of the fear—all she could think about was going to bed with a man she had known less than a week—a man who was engaged to marry another woman. There was definitely something wrong with her!

His hand was moving tenderly over her head now, smoothing her hair away from her damp cheeks and her temples. He was so kind. So gentle. So utterly, quietly masculine....

"Would you mind getting me a couple more aspirin and a glass of water?" she asked with only a hint of the desperation she felt.

"Look, why don't you just put on a raincoat over your nightgown and I'll drive you to my doctor. He can check you over, probably give you something a lot more effective than aspirin."

"I don't—"

But in the end, she did. There was no arguing with incapacitating pain. Nor was there any arguing with a determined man.

Chloe insisted on dressing, but Quint was just as insistent. He laid out her clothes and stood just outside in the hall while she finished in the bathroom and pulled on a pair of beige silk slacks and a matching silk sweater—hardly practical for a rainy November morning, but then, it was all she could do to get herself dressed, never mind suitably dressed.

He also insisted on carrying her to the car, and Chloe didn't bother to argue. All she wanted was relief from the debilitating pain, and assurance that it was nothing life-threatening.

"Promise me something," she said when he had settled her in his car and climbed in beside her.

"Sure. Your seat belt snug enough?"

"Yes, for goodness' sake, my seat belt is just fine! Now listen—I want you to promise me that if—well, if anything happens to me in the next few days, you won't send word of my—of anything to Florida. Is that clear?"

"Clear?" He looked at her as if he feared for her sanity—as well he might, she thought helplessly. All the same, *something* was dreadfully wrong with her. She could be gravely ill. Maybe even terminally ill. But if she couldn't be assured of having a simple, dignified obituary, untainted by Brice and his common-law wife, and her father's misdeeds, she would damned well refuse to die!

"Well? Do I have your promise?"

"Maybe you'd better get in the back and lie down. It's not far, but—"

"There's nothing wrong with me! I mean, there is, but— What I mean is, there's nothing wrong with my mind." Her hands knotted in her lap as she stared out at the gray, featureless landscape.

"Mmm-hmm," Quint murmured, glancing at her cautiously from the corner of his eye.

Chloe sighed. How in the world could a woman of her age and experience wind up in such a royal mess? She had been made a fool of before by experts, but not one of them had done such a complete job of it as she had, all by herself.

"I expect you're wishing you'd never laid eyes on me," she ventured after several minutes had passed.

"Under the circumstances, maybe...."

She sighed again, hyperventilating. A stress symptom, or some such nonsense. But she wasn't stressed; she was quite simply dying of a brain tumor. The fact that no one—other than a second cousin she hadn't seen in several months—would even care was neither here nor there.

"Well, at least you're honest," she grumbled.

"I like to think so," Quint allowed modestly as he pulled into a small but attractively designed cypress complex that, according to the sign at the entrance, housed two medical practices, a pharmacy and an optometrist's office. "I called while you were in the bathroom. They're expecting you."

Whiplash. She felt like a fraud. "I always thought whiplash was one of those imaginary conditions dreamed up by lawyers for milking insurance companies," she said on the drive home. "All those poor victims with braces on their necks and dollar signs in their eyes. I don't even have a brace—my neck's just fine."

The doctor had examined her quite thoroughly before explaining about the network of nerves at the base of her skull, which were just now reacting to the punishment inflicted on them when her head had been flung sharply forward and then backward again.

"Usually happens about five days after a wreck—sometimes a week, sometimes just a few days. Hurts like the very devil, but it's just a matter of spasming muscles putting pressure on those nerves I told you about. I'm gonna give you something for pain, and a muscle relaxant. But I'll have to caution you against using heavy machinery while you're taking the stuff. No streakin' off across country on your bulldozer or roarin' around town on a backhoe, y'hear now?"

Feeling vastly relieved, Chloe had promised to call if she had any more trouble. At first she'd been put off by the physician's jeans, red flannel shirt and rather casual manner, but his credentials had checked out. Half the certificates gracing the walls of his small office were from first-rate medical schools, the other half being for record fish he had caught over the years. Evidently golf was not his game.

She was feeling drowsy and much more relaxed by the time they reached Quinton's home, but he made her eat something before she went to bed.

"I'm not hungry," she insisted.

"Tea and toast, then. My Mama used to swear by tea and toast."

Grudgingly she had allowed him to bring it up to her bedroom, where he had stayed until she'd finished the lot—scalding water with a tea bag in it, and two slices of cold toast.

Tomorrow, she vowed as she drifted off to sleep... Tomorrow she would call Buster and see about making a deal on her car. Tomorrow, she would call Ginny and tell her she was on her way.

But "tomorrow" turned out to be forty-six hours later.

Chapter Six

Various sections of her body seemed to come alive as Chloe stared up at the ceiling, watching patterns of dancing sunlight that were reflected from something outside the window. According to the sun, it was still daylight. According to the clock, it was a bit after nine. And since it got dark about five-thirty these days, that meant 9:00 a.m., not 9:00 p.m.

But it had been just about nine forty-five when they had left to visit the doctor. And raining hard.

All right, so the clock had stopped. More to the point, she was starving, she had to go to the bathroom rather badly—and her headache was considerably better. Still there, but much, much improved.

Cautiously levering herself up to a sitting position, Chloe grabbed the edge of the bedside table and waited for the spots to swim out of her vision. Good Lord, she felt weak! And grungy. She needed a shower—or better yet, a long, warm soak, a shampoo, and an enormous breakfast.

In the hallway, with negligee and fresh underwear clutched in her hand, Chloe paused, hearing the murmur of voices from downstairs. Or rather, a single voice. Quint's.

Very quietly, she closed the bathroom door behind her and began running water into the old-fashioned bathtub. She felt a small qualm of guilt as she realized he had probably stayed home from work to make sure she was all right. Even so, she could do without his interference at the moment. As soon as she felt a bit more human, she would tell him to go back to his office, that she would be perfectly fine. And once he'd gone, she would call Buster and get on with the business of selling her car.

On second thought, the first thing she would do was make herself something to eat. Anything, as long as there was plenty of it.

Slowly, as she ducked her hair under the water and lathered it with Quint's shampoo, Chloe began remembering. The first thought that streaked through her mind was that her hairdresser would have had apoplexy if he could see her washing her hair in bathwater.

Bathwater. Bathroom. Something flickered in her mind, leaving behind a fragmented image of Quint's propping her against the bathroom wall and saying, "Call me the minute you're finished, you hear? And if you start to feel dizzy..."

She must have been dreaming. Those pills she'd taken had knocked her for a loop. Surely she'd only dreamed she saw Quint sprawled out in that miserable bentwood rocker, his long legs stretched halfway across the room and his unshaven jaw slack as he snored ever so softly.

Ducking her head under the water again, she swished her hair and then sat up and felt for a towel.

Twenty minutes later, she opened the door and walked head-on into what felt like a stone wall. "Oh, I—"

"Watch it!" Quint reached out to steady her before she could fall back, his expression thunderous. Startled, Chloe saw only his anger, missing completely the concern that had brought him upstairs on the run the moment he had hung up the phone to hear water gurgling down the drain.

"Why the devil didn't you call me if you wanted to go to the bathroom?" he demanded.

Had he gone mad? Chloe's staring eyes slowly lost their focus as she became aware of several things at once. Aware of the contrast of strength and gentleness in the hands that were gripping her upper arms. Of the crow's-feet bracketing a pair of darkest amber eyes. Of the tantalizing glimpse of a full, firm lower lip under the soft brush of his thick mustache—and the enticing scent of him that made her senses reel.

Not only her senses...

"Hey, don't pass out on me!" He swept her up, and Chloe's fragile self-control snapped.

"Would you *mind*? I am perfectly capable of—"

"Lying flat on your backside until I get you sorted out," he finished for her.

Bristling, she sat up straight—or as straight as one can sit when suspended five feet off the floor in the arms of a towering Ukrainian secret agent. "Please don't think I don't appreciate your concern," she seethed, "but if you don't put me down this very instant, I'm going to—I'm going to sock you on the jaw!"

At the head of the stairs, Quint stopped dead in his tracks to stare down at her. And then, to her utter amazement, he burst out laughing.

All she could do was hold on as he carried her down the stairs and into the living room, where he lowered her onto the wing chair and drew an ottoman under her feet.

"There," he pronounced, as if he had accomplished a minor miracle. "Back in the land of the living, at last. Hang on a minute and I'll bring you some soup and crackers."

If it was on a par with his coffee, it would be something lumpy, lukewarm and canned—probably a vegetable mush. On the other hand, canned soup was better than nothing. A whole lot better.

However, the soup, when it arrived, was steaming, fragrant, and obviously homemade. Quint arranged a lapboard over the arms of the chair and placed the tray upon it. He had set it carefully with a Wedgwood soup plate, a tarnished sterling soupspoon, a paper napkin and an unwrapped tube of saltines. In a water tumbler he had placed a sprig of holly and the battered stem of a stunted chrysanthemum.

Chloe felt like weeping for no good reason at all. "This looks wonderful," she said, reaching for the spoon.

"Does that mean you're glad you didn't haul off and plant me one on the jaw?"

His eyes were twinkling when she looked up at him, but with a mouthful of vegetable-beef ambrosia, she was in no position to reply.

"Janet brought the soup over yesterday. Her mother made it."

"Yesterday?" Chloe frowned, but kept right on eating. "I don't remember...."

"You were dead to the world. I roused you a couple of times and got you to drink a few swallows of milk with your pills, but—"

"Milk! Good Lord, why on earth would you do that?"

Quint sat on the chair opposite hers, one leg slung horizontally across the other in what Chloe was coming to consider a typical attitude. He was a large man. A very masculine man, she thought absently. A very, *very* masculine man.

"Well, hell," replied the very masculine man. "I couldn't just let you starve, could I? I figured that, semiconscious, you could handle a few swallows of milk better than you could deal with a bucket of chicken or a cheeseburger and fries."

Something was wrong here. As soon as she finished her soup, she was going to get to the bottom of it. "At least it's stopped raining," she said as she scooped up the last succulent shred of beef.

"Stopped yesterday. Cleared off about the middle of the morning."

Yesterday. Then that meant... "Oh, Lord, I slept right through yesterday, didn't I? I can't believe it!" Setting aside her empty bowl, she suddenly wished she hadn't eaten quite so much, or so fast.

Quint grinned, and to her own annoyance, Chloe could not help but notice the striking contrast of gleaming white teeth under the thick, dark mustache, or the way his cheeks creased all the way up to his high, Slavic-looking cheekbones.

"Sure did," he drawled. "Yesterday, half of the day before, and most of today. All in all, you had a pretty hefty nap, honey."

Dazedly she shook her head. "That's impossible. No, I just wouldn't have done that—I never sleep more than seven hours a night. Not even that much since—for a long time. You're teasing me, aren't you?"

The grin became a gentle smile, and Chloe immediately interpreted the warmth in his eyes as pity. She turned away, wanting to delay the moment of truth.

"So the doctor lied to me," she whispered.

"He did *what*?"

She stared unseeingly at a shriveled cactus on a table in front of the window. Whiplash! They'd both been trying to spare her feelings, thinking perhaps that just because she looked fragile, she would collapse under the strain.

But Chloe had learned the hard way that she was a lot tougher than she looked. "All right, let me have it straight out," she said, bracing herself for one more crippling blow. She could deal with this. It was simply a matter of putting it in perspective. "I'm dying, aren't I?"

Quint looked so stunned, she could hardly credit him with putting on an act. "What the hell are you talking about?"

"Look, I don't know just how much your Doctor Whatsis told you, but I have to know the truth, Quint.

I'm not afraid of it." Only terrified. Only totally pet-rified. "I'm not alone—not at all. Oh, no— You see, I have this cousin in Maryland—that's Ginny—she's a CPA, and terribly bright. And I was actually on my way to visit her when all this happened, so she's prob-ably wondering what happened to me.... Well, I didn't actually tell her when I was coming, but all the same... So if you don't mind, I'd like to try to get—"

"Chloe." His voice cut through her frantic ram-blings like a hot knife through butter. "Just hush up and let me bring you your medicine, okay? Then if you want to talk, I'll listen."

She began shaking her head from side to side. "Oh, no. Ooooh, no, you don't. No more knockout pills, thank you very much."

"Doctor Whats—that is, Doc McCall doesn't deal in knockout drops. These are pain pills and a muscle relaxant. I checked with him when you snoozed through the first few meals."

"Just forget it, all right? Pain, I can take. What I can't take is not knowing what's going on. I don't *ever* want to be in a position where everyone knows the truth but me. Do you understand?"

He was watching her as if he expected her to sud-denly fly up to the ceiling and start circling the chan-delier. "No. I can't say I do understand."

She gulped air and expelled it in a long sigh while her nails grooved half-moons in her palms. "Look, it's quite simple. I have no intention of making a specta-cle of myself by—by dying among strangers. It's—it's just not dignified. And I certainly don't intend to take any pills that are going to knock me out so that I waste what little time I do have left." She swallowed and stared hard at the dusty, shrunken cactus. "Uh—how much time do I have, do you happen to know?"

Silence.

Chloe couldn't look at him for fear of what she might read in his eyes. Instead, she lifted her gaze beyond the poor dead houseplant, through the smeared windowpane and beyond, filling her soul with the beauty of a golden water oak that danced gently against a sky of purest cobalt. Tears formed in her eyes and spilled out over her cheeks. So much loveliness all around her. So little time left to enjoy it.

Sniffling, she swiped at her eyes with her crumpled paper napkin. Oh, how she abhorred self-pity. It was so... messy! At least she wasn't wearing mascara.

One look at Quint through a hedge of wet lashes was enough to let her know that he had missed none of her maudlin display. Not a gulp, a sniffle or a whimper.

Damn.

There he sat, like a muscular, hirsute Buddha. Those all-seeing eyes of his weren't missing a trick— from her quivering insides to her soap-dulled hair, to her red, shiny nose.

"Oh, for pity's sake, can't a woman even have a moment of privacy to contemplate her own mortality without some smart-mouthed Ukrainian fertilizer spy butting in?"

After a single moment of astonishment, Quint burst out laughing again.

If Chloe could have got herself out from behind a lapful of dishes, she would have crowned him! Of all the heartless, unfeeling creeps! "You're really enjoying this, aren't you? It delights you to see me—to watch while I—"

He sobered instantly. "You want to know what delights me? I'll tell you. It's watching you dig into your food like you really enjoy it. It's watching the color return to your face—and I don't mean those purple shadows under your eyes."

Shocked into silence, Chloe lifted a hand to touch the face that was utterly devoid of cosmetics, devoid of the Shadow-Out she had used under her eyes for so long to mask the signs of too little sleep and too much stress.

"As for what I see," he continued, "I see a beautiful woman who's either gutsy as hell or scared witless—maybe both. A woman who's down on her luck and too damned proud to ask for help. I see a woman who could do with a friend, but who doesn't know how to accept friendship when it's offered."

Chloe's response was a long time in coming. Only now was she beginning to realize how far out on a mental limb she had climbed. "You mean I'm not really seriously ill?" she ventured. Somehow, she knew the truth even before he confirmed it.

"You're not seriously ill. Hurting, yes. And if I were to attempt a guess, I'd say you've been through some pretty rough times lately. I suspect you're running. But pain and pills on top of too much stress don't make for clear thinking. A word of advice from a friend—why don't you relax and give it a few more days before you start trying to figure out your next move?"

Quint waited. He didn't expect her to corroborate his guess, but he knew he couldn't be far off the mark.

He'd done a lot of thinking since he'd pulled her out of that car—too damn much for his own peace of mind.

The woman got to him. She was beautiful, sure, but he was too old to be taken in by mere physical beauty. Part of the trouble was that she was needy as hell. He'd always been a sucker for lame ducks, as Janet was always pointing out.

And that was another thing—Janet. How the hell could a man lust after one woman the day he got himself engaged to marry another one? In fact, how in all conscience could he lust after a woman who was hurting, broke, and more alone than any creature he'd seen in a long, long time? What kind of an unprincipled creep did that make him?

At least he hadn't done anything about it. Now, all he had to do was find the willpower to send her on her way before he did something they would both regret.

Dropping his right foot to the floor, he leaned forward, arms braced on his thighs. "Chloe," he said earnestly, "I want you to promise me you won't even *think* about leaving until you're completely recovered."

So much for willpower.

She looked everywhere but at him. "Look, I do appreciate all you've done for me. And I know, honestly I do, that there's nothing seriously wrong with me. I don't know why I fell apart like that. Normally, I'm the most levelheaded person you'd ever meet."

"Sure. I know that, honey. It was the medicine on top of the shock, on top of whatever put those shadows under your eyes in the first place." He could see her begin to withdraw before he had even finished speaking, and he held up a hand, palm out. "Okay, okay... None of my business, right? Just promise me one thing, Chloe: you'll stay until you're back in fighting trim. And if you need a friend, I'm here."

He thought she was going to cloud up and rain again, but she managed to pull together a smile. A little shaky, but so damned beautiful it made his belly ache.

"I knew that," she said. The smile spread to her eyes, putting him in mind of a shaft of sunlight in a cloudy gray sky. "By the way," she went on in that tremulous voice that right from the first had reminded him of fancy houses and stiff-necked butlers and little girls in white gloves and black patent shoes. "Did you know I had you pegged for a Ukrainian fertilizer spy?"

His right foot, which he'd just slung across his left thigh again, hit the floor with a solid thump. Staring at her with his thick brows drawn into a frown of concern, he said, "Uh—we might want to check with Doc McCall about the aftereffects of that medication. Maybe you're pushing things a little, getting up so soon...."

Chloe laughed and reached for the tube of crackers. "It's not a side effect. Don't worry. Didn't I tell you about my road game? Whenever I'm driving any distance, I pass the time by making up stories about towns I pass through and people I see. You were the only thing on that particular stretch of highway to create about, so I used you. As a matter of fact, there was a logger for a while—I had him up to his ears in a smuggling ring, but he turned off before I figured out how to lure him into a trap."

"Lady, you are a horse of an altogether different color," Quint drawled softly—that slow, familiar grin spreading over his face. "So now I'm a Ukrainian spy, hmm?"

"It's partly your car, but mostly your cheekbones," Chloe explained, wishing she'd never brought it up. Now he *would* think she was demented. The last time she had shared one of her "creations" with anyone, she'd been attending some boring compulsory social affair with her father because his current wife had come down with the flu at the last minute. He had given her a look that queried her sanity and told her to stand up straight and stop giggling like a silly schoolgirl. She'd been seventeen at the time.

"Is there any Ukrainian blood in your family?" she asked, discreetly dusting cracker crumbs off her bosom.

"Not to my knowledge. English and Scots, mostly—although there was my great-great-grandmother on my father's side. Her name, according to family records, was Anna Little Crow. That sound Ukrainian to you?"

Chloe laughed, and Quint rose and gathered up her tray. "Be a good girl and stay put, will you? I'll bring you some coffee."

"Lots of milk, please," she called after him, and laughed again, feeling weak, but immeasurably cheerful for some strange reason. Nothing had really changed. She was still broke—not only broke, but in debt. She was still a few hundred miles from her destination, and for all she knew, Ginny could have moved, or married, or done any of a dozen other things that would complicate her own plans.

But right now, none of that seemed to matter. Chloe knew she was reacting to weakness from too many days in bed, too little food—and probably from the pent-up strain of the past few years. She'd held up all through both ordeals, never losing control, because there had been so much to do; so many endless, tedious details to be seen to in both cases.

Held together by miles and miles of red tape, she thought with a slightly hysterical urge to laugh. Take away the tape and everything starts coming apart.

"Hey, you want some peanut butter and pretzels with your coffee?" Quint called from the kitchen.

Peanut butter and pretzels? She was in questionable shape, but she wasn't that far gone! "No thanks," she called back.

Actually, she was in pretty good shape. She had a place to stay—for a few more days, at least—and even a possible way to repay Quint for his hospitality. She had a car that, even wrecked, was worth enough to pay her way to Keedysville and keep her until she could find a job. And she had a cousin who happened to be one of her favorite people. No, she certainly wasn't in bad shape.

All in all she was in wonderful shape, she concluded, as she watched Quint's progress through the dining room with a tray that held coffee, a small pitcher of milk, a sugar bowl, a box of pretzels and a jar of peanut butter. "Oh, hell, the cups," he muttered, and turned back.

Chloe felt a smile start somewhere deep inside her and gradually spread to the outside. What a wonderful man. What a wonderful, unpolished, unselfish, imperfect, generous—and sexy—man.

* * *

Chloe firmly rejected Quint's suggestion that she rest in bed for the remainder of the day. She refused point-blank to take her medicine. Not so much as an aspirin would cross her lips until she got herself in hand again—she'd made herself a promise.

He argued, of course. He was good at that.

But for once, Chloe was adamant. "If I'm suffering," she told him, "I want to know precisely how *much* I'm suffering. How can I tell when I've recovered if I'm snowed under with medication?"

"Did anyone ever tell you you were as stubborn as a cross-eyed mule?"

"No. No one's ever told me I'm stubborn for the simple reason that I'm not."

"Ha! And I'm a two-headed toe dancer!"

Playfully Chloe allowed her gaze to slide down his brown flannel shirt and faded jeans, all the way to his size-twelve split-leather moccasins. "This is your practice costume, I take it. I do hope your tutu's pink—it would look heavenly with your dark mustache."

With mock ferocity, he clasped her face between his hands, and suddenly the air went out of the room. Chloe felt as if she were suspended in a vacuum, in a magnetic field of enormous power. Before she could even think, she had covered his hands with her own, and now she was trapped, her eyes clinging to his while her skin burned at his touch.

Seconds ticked by, marked only by the raspy, uneven sound of breathing. Hers? His?

Theirs. She fancied she could feel a pulse beating in the tip of his finger on her temple, but then she realized that it was probably her own. And it was racing out of control.

There was all the time in the world to get out of his way, if she'd had either the strength or the desire.

Chloe had neither. Just as his face went out of focus above hers, she shut her eyes tightly and uttered a small whimper, born partly of protest, but mostly of need.

He tasted like cold November rain and hot, sweet coffee. The feel of his mustache crushed softly against her cheek and upper lip brought course after course of lightning streaking down through her body.

Somewhere in the detached part of her brain that was still functioning, she was aware that this was a perfect kiss—that no other kiss she had ever received had come even faintly close to having this effect on her.

Quint held her pressed tightly against him so that she could feel his strength, his warmth, the shuddering beat of his heart and his rising passion. And God help her, she was with him every step of the way.

He lifted his head ever so slightly, and she rose on tiptoe to follow him. "Please," she whispered, her eyes pleading for him to stop this madness, her heart pleading for it never to end.

With a softly uttered profanity, he stepped back, his eyes as impenetrable as the darkest night. For one small eternity, Chloe hung suspended in space.

And then she landed back on earth with a thump. Smoothing her hair, she searched wildly for something to say, as if mere words could negate what had just occurred. "Yes, well—I promised Janet I'd make some suggestions about…" *About what? Janet who?* "Uh—about the dining room."

Quint's Adam's apple bobbed as he swallowed, and then he nodded vigorously. "Yeah, sure. The dining room. That's right nice of you, if it's not too much— uh… Janet's not— That is, I'm not…"

He turned and strode away, leaving her clutching the back of the sofa. As her world slowly righted itself, Chloe stared after him.

It wasn't possible, of course. It was the medicine. A muscle relaxant was bound to have some effect on the central nervous system.

Her brain had shut down momentarily; that was all it was. Either that, or she'd been caught up in a Kansas cyclone that had dumped her out in the Land of Oz.

Chapter Seven

It *was* a rooster! Chloe sat up in bed and listened for the sound that had awakened her. She didn't have to wait long. Leaping out of bed, she groaned as an assortment of muscles protested sharply, and then she stumbled to the window, throwing it open to a coral-streaked sky.

"Ur-*urr-urrrrh*!"

"Coooo-hoooo," came the soft response.

"Well, good morning to you, too, darlings—wherever and whatever you are."

Five minutes later she was downstairs, wearing only her gown and peignoir, a white cotton cardigan and a pair of gray satin slippers. Hardly her most fashionable attire, but then, this was an emergency. She'd been hearing—or dreaming she heard—these same strange sounds ever since she'd arrived here, and this time, she fully intended to get to the bottom of whatever was doing all the crowing and cooing.

For as long as she could remember—or at least for the first dozen or so years of her life—Chloe had wanted a pet. She'd asked at various times for baby chicks, ducklings, squirrels, monkeys, ponies, and any number of cats and dogs whose beguiling portraits had appeared in the pound's adopt-a-pet advertisements.

For all the good it had done her. Poultry was out of the question, according to both her father and the housekeeper. Squirrels spread rabies. Monkeys—well, she couldn't quite recall what had been wrong with monkeys, but the rest had been equally impossible. The plain truth was, they simply had not cared for animals.

Her mother had given her an enormous saltwater aquarium when she was seven, but the fish had died, and when she'd refused to allow the man from the pet shop to remove them, certain they were only resting, her father had gotten rid of the whole thing.

As solace, she'd been given a purebred, half-grown Afghan, which had gone through the house like a tornado on his first day in residence, and been banished to the chauffeur's garage apartment, which, of course, had been off-limits to her.

"Here, chicken, chicken, chicken, nice chicken," she crooned softly as she crept down the back steps onto the leaf-covered lawn. The crisp air was sweet with the breath of a thousand pines, and she drew her lightweight cardigan together over her breast and held out the slice of bread she'd brought to lure the chicken—or whatever—from his tree. "Wouldn't you like a nice slice of toast for breakfast? It's whole grain, you'll love it." She tried whistling, but it had never been a particular talent of hers.

"Please come out, chicken. You don't have to be afraid of me, I promise you. Look, I'll just leave your breakfast here at the foot of the steps and you can come out and eat when you're ready, all right?" She tossed the bread and then scanned the overgrown shrubs and the edge of the woods for a sign of movement, slowly backing up, a step at a time.

Suddenly the door behind her opened just as the back of her ankle struck the bottom step, and she sat down hard.

"Hey, watch it," Quint called out, hurrying to her side.

"You watch it! How dare you sneak up on me that way!" Her dignity was smarting—not to mention her behind.

"Sorry, I didn't mean to startle you. I just couldn't figure out what you were doing out here, or who you were talking to." He looked around, and then back at her.

"I was talking to the birds," Chloe snapped, and then wished she'd had the good sense to remain silent. It was a perfectly reasonable thing to do; still, it didn't *sound* particularly intelligent.

"Did Urk get you up? I'm sorry about that. He used to hang around the loft with the homers, but then I got to feeding him peanuts on the back porch. I'm sorry he bothered you. I'll catch him when he goes to roost tonight and shut him up in the barn."

Chloe stood and unconsciously rubbed her backside. "Please don't bother on my account," she said, aware of a good many things that had escaped her a moment before—such as the cold; such as the thinness of her garments; such as the way Quint was staring at her, as if he suspected her of having had a relapse.

"Look, could we go inside? Your—Urk, or whatever you called him, obviously isn't interested in whole-grain bread, but it was the only thing I could think of."

Quint grinned, looking surprisingly boyish for a man nearing his fortieth year. "Hang on, I'll be back in two shakes," he told her, wheeling away to disappear inside the kitchen.

She still hadn't managed to close her mouth by the time he reappeared. "Watch this," he said conspiratorially, drumming on the porch railing with his fingernails.

"Ur-urr-urrrrhhh!" came the immediate response.

Astonished, Chloe watched as a small bundle of glistening red-and-black feathers flew across the clearing and landed on the railing within a couple of feet of where they stood. She stepped back reflexively, even as she admired the picture-perfect bird that preened and strutted before her.

"Knew that would get to you, old man. Here, have a peanut and say hello to our guest." Quint opened his palm and the bantam rooster ducked his head, his fiery red comb bobbing furiously as he gobbled up both halves of the nut he'd been offered.

"The old guy's spoiled rotten," Quint remarked, grinning more widely than ever. "He's older than a rooster has any right to be, but the little devil is too damned stubborn to die. Last of the flock. I gave up getting him hens years ago, because as soon as they laid a clutch of eggs, they'd go to roosting on the ground, and that was the end of 'em.''

"Oh, no," Chloe answered softly, edging closer to the preening bird.

"Sorry. Chickens aren't known for their intellect."

"Doesn't he get lonely?"

"Not as long as he can strut his stuff in front of chrome bumpers, hubcaps, or the old piece of mirror I shoved up under the porch. The guy's got a heavy Narcissus complex. The homers still hang around, and half the time, I think he believes he's a pigeon."

"Pigeon. That's the other thing I heard, then." She was shivering hard by now, but she was far too fascinated with this rare glimpse of farm life—or whatever—to go inside.

"My dad used to raise racing homers. There're still a few of them left, and since this is home..."

"I suppose this is what Janet meant when she said you take in strays," she said through chattering teeth, and Quint gave her a look of concern. "Do you think I could feed him a peanut?"

"If you do it before you turn into a block of ice," he replied, handing her the rest of his supply. "But these guys aren't strays. This is as much their home as it is mine."

While a watchful Quint rested his lean hips against the porch railing, Chloe set about luring the rooster to eat from her hand. It took all of thirty seconds.

"I think you'd better put it down in front of him," Quint suggested, but she didn't want to do that. She wanted him to eat from her hand.

"I'd rather—" she began, and then she gasped at the shock of a hard beak driving into her tender palm.

Quint snatched up her hand and examined it, after shooing the bird off the railing. "He didn't break the skin, did he? God, I'm sorry, honey—I should've known. My hand's so tough I never even feel it, but I should have known better than to let you risk getting eaten alive by that old panhandler."

"It startled me, that's all," answered Chloe, who was far more conscious of Quint's warm hand cupping hers than she was of the momentary pain. "I should've been prepared."

"His beak's worn down so it'll hardly close anymore, but all the same..."

Quint led her inside as if she were still an invalid, and Chloe lost no time in extricating herself from his solicitous embrace. "I'm sorry if I woke you," she said, instinctively moving so that the table stood between them.

"I was awake. Actually, I was wondering if maybe something could be done about my room—that is, while you're making notes about the rest of the house, I thought..." His voice dwindled off as he continued to gaze at her.

"You thought?" She tried not to stare at the broad strip of hairy chest revealed between the two sides of a navy flannel shirt. Did the man have no sense of propriety whatsoever? Couldn't he even manage to button his shirt before presenting himself in public?

Chloe had seen men in bathing trunks and tennis shorts, and even in the nude—she had been married, after all. Yet Quinton Stevens, standing barefoot and bare chested in the middle of his kitchen in the gray half-light of dawn, had a more profound effect on her than Brice had had on their honeymoon, wearing no more than a black silk robe, a pair of Geoffrey Beene slippers and a generous splash of cologne.

It had happened. She was finally losing touch with reality.

"Forget it," Quint mumbled.

"Forget—? Oh." Years of deportment classes and more years of practice came into play, and she recovered nicely. "I'm sorry, Quinton. If I appear a bit dense, it's only because I don't usually function well before I've had my morning coffee. You were speaking of my making notes on your bedroom? The decor, you mean?"

His mustache twitched, and she could see the laughter in his eyes even before she heard it in his voice. "Yeah, I guess that's what you call it. I build houses. I leave the rest of that stuff to someone else."

"I believe it," Chloe murmured under her breath. But he heard it and grinned all the more.

"I think we both need some coffee," he agreed, and while he was making it, at his usual double strength, he went on to say, "Seriously, Chloe—if you meant what you said about doing something to the house, then maybe you'd be so kind as to take a look at my bedroom."

Would you care to see my collection of etchings, my dear? I hung them in my boudoir for safekeeping, so if you'll step this way?

"There's a room that opens off it that Janet might like," Quint was saying. "How would it be to sort of do 'em up together? Same color and all that?"

Not even a pitcher of ice water poured over her head would have been quite so effective. Janet and Quint.

Quint and Janet. Mr. and Mrs. Quinton Bond—*Stevens*!

Mr. and Mrs. Quinton *Stevens*. The man might have questionable taste in women, but he was definitely no wimp.

"Yes. Of course. I mean, that sounds reasonable enough." She and Brice had not shared a room, nor had her father with any of his wives, since her mother. But somehow, she would have expected a man like Quint to insist that his wife share his bedroom.

Dammit, just quit that! Just because he happens to be the sexiest man you've ever laid eyes on—just because he's warm and kind and funny and gentle . . .

Chloe lifted her head proudly, just as if she weren't dressed for a midnight fire drill—just as if her hair weren't streaming like wet rope down over her shoulders. "After you leave to go to work, I'll look over the two rooms and jot down my suggestions, but now, if you'll excuse me—" She managed to reach the door just as the coffee maker gurgled one last gasp and sighed over a job well-done.

Quint pulled out a chair. "Hey, come on back and have some coffee before you go to work. You said yourself—"

"I *know* what I said!" So much for beating a graceful retreat.

"Head still bothering you?" Quint placed a full mug of steaming, fragrant, life-giving caffeine before her, and Chloe restrained herself from throwing it at him.

What was happening to her? Ever since she'd landed in this bucolic backwoods, she had consistently overreacted to every single thing the man said or did. It was not only out of character, it was downright gauche!

Quint left for work, and Chloe sipped her second cup of diluted coffee and nibbled thoughtfully on a slice of toast. What was it her nanny, Anna, always used to say when she'd caught some childhood disease like measles or chicken pox? "When you start getting cranky, it's a good sign you're on the mend."

Sweet, amenable, docile little Chloe. Dutiful daughter, dutiful wife, dutiful...idiot! She must be mending fast, then, because at the rate she was biting off heads, she'd be able to get a job as the lead lion with the first circus that came to town.

By the end of the day Chloe had made several sketches and scribbled copious notes on a pad she found half hidden under the heap of papers on Quint's dining-room table. In the process, she'd learned that the small Victorian desk in the living room was reserved for personal correspondence, household bills and charitable solicitations, while the dining-room table, china cabinets and buffet served as an extension of Stevens-Bond Development, Inc.

In spite of the chaotic appearance, there was a certain order in the piles of papers in both rooms—nothing a good secretary couldn't get through in a few weeks' time.

As for the rest of the clutter, she had decided right away that the glass-fronted cabinet that was crammed full of lovely old china, crystal and tarnished hollowware, would make a perfect bookcase, thus enabling her to get rid of the stacks of books on the floor and on every other available surface.

It seemed that someone in the family either had been, or still was, a voracious reader with wide-ranging interests. There were even a few books on civil engineering and marine biology among the Colonial history tomes and the usual cloak-and-dagger classics.

She might have known her Mr. Y would go in for those. If she were going to be around long enough, she'd have enjoyed nothing better than to settle back on a cold rainy evening and share a warm drink and a chilling story.

But . . . she wasn't.

After a brief pause to raid the refrigerator sometime about noon, Chloe moved on to the old kitchen. With its darkened paneling and its high ceiling, it could easily be converted into a charming, informal dining room. A thorough scrubbing, followed by a wash of thin white paint would lighten and brighten the stained pine walls, in spite of a dearth of windows. In fact, the back door that had probably opened out onto a kitchen garden at one time, could be made into French doors that would open onto a small patio and an herb garden to catch the morning dew and the evening sunset.

For someone who was merely passing through, Chloe realized she was taking an entirely too personal interest in future arrangements.

Sighing, she curled up in the enormous leather chair that dwarfed the late Camilla Stevens's more delicate furniture, and began writing out her suggestions in the flawless Palmer penmanship that had been drilled into her a quarter of a century before by Sister Ursula. As her enthusiasm grew, the dots over her *i*'s became dashes, and the crosses over her *t*'s fell short of the mark.

The crammed pages fell unheeded to the floor, and not until she heard Urk drumming on the porch railing for peanuts did she stop to flex her fingers and look down at all she'd done.

Good heavens, where had the time gone? She'd planned to spend an hour, at most, making a few recommendations, and then get on with her own pressing business. Now she'd wasted an entire day!

How many times had she traipsed back up those stairs to check the number of windows in a room, or the width of the hall? She had gone into every single bedroom on the second floor, with the exception of the master bedroom and the room beside it.

Somehow, in spite of her promise to Quint, Chloe had not been able to bring herself to invade his personal territory. Surely that was Janet's responsibility? It wasn't as if she were a legitimate decorator; her only experience was having lived through more upheavals in her own home than she cared to remember, as each of her father's wives had sought to put her stamp on his domain.

Brice's home had been untouchable. He had let her know right from the first that being his wife gave her no rights at all where his home was concerned. She was to manage his social engagements, see that his clothes were kept in readiness, and on rare occasions when he wasn't too tired, grace his bed. Other than that, her role was a public one.

With an expression of annoyance, Chloe dropped her pad and pen and stretched. The bruise on her forearm was now a livid shade of purple with yellow borders, and the one on her shoulder a purplish red, but the rest of her assorted aches and pains were subsiding nicely. She had taken two aspirin after breakfast and nothing since, and her headache was barely noticeable.

There was just time before Quint got home to try Ginny again and call Buster's garage. Poor Quint. She suspected he'd neglected his work shamefully since she'd been here—especially during her embarrassing sleep marathon.

She dialed her cousin's number for the third time that day, to no avail. By now she was beginning to grow just a wee bit uneasy. It wouldn't be the first time Ginny had taken off on the spur of the moment to some wildly exotic place. A CPA by profession, she was supposed to be staid and predictable, but Ginny Hathaway was about as predictable as a waterspout.

Buster's line was still busy—she suspected he took the phone off the hook when he didn't want to be bothered. Before she could get on with the next item on her agenda, Chloe heard Quint drive up. He had driven his muddy red pickup truck instead of the Ford, and if the thing had ever possessed a muffler, it had long since expired.

"Will Janet be coming over tonight?" she asked almost before he could shut the door behind him. He was wearing a tan windbreaker over black corduroys and a brown flannel shirt—hardly traditional office wear, but then Gumtree Corners, as she had learned the neighborhood was called, was hardly Tallahassee. Or even Williamston.

"Not tonight. She's planning to have another go at Adamson over dinner. Once she's got her teeth into something like that riverside track of his, she can't seem to let go."

Chloe had heard enough to know that Janet was envisioning a large shopping center on the Roanoke River near the intersection of highways 64 and 17, while Quint considered that the existing shopping center was sufficient, and that a residential park would be the best use if the property had to be developed at all.

Janet, she had discovered, was a very determined lady; but she rather thought that Quint, in his quiet, understated way, would be more than a match for her. "Then shall I cook us something? I didn't look in the freezer to see what there was—I thought the two of you would be going out and I could make myself a sandwich."

"How about the two of us going out? You look like you've been overdoing it today. A good hot meal and an early night is exactly what you need."

Even knowing she was overreacting, she couldn't stop herself. "I have *not* been overdoing it, and what I *need* is a *sandwich*! On a tray in my room! And if that doesn't suit you, then perhaps it's time I moved out."

Neither of them had mentioned that unexpected kiss, but for some reason, that was all she could think of now. The very air that hovered between them seemed to sizzle. Chloe had been able to forget the taste and the feel of Quint's mouth on hers for long periods of time during the day—just as long as she kept herself going at breakneck speed. But the moment she relaxed—or the moment Quint entered the room where she was—something inside her began to twist tighter and tighter, like the mainspring of an overwound clock.

Abruptly she announced, "I'll just go upstairs and pack, and then if you would be so kind as to—"

Two steps and he was practically breathing down her throat, his eyes narrowed to slivers of obsidian. His voice, when it came, was dangerously soft. "Easy there, girl. Don't get all riled up. You're not under any threat. You want a sandwich on a tray? Fine. You just go on upstairs and climb into bed, and I'll bring it up to you. You want milk or coffee with it?"

Chloe ground her teeth. What she wanted was—what she *wanted* . . .

She *didn't know* what she wanted. At least, she didn't dare admit, even to herself, what it was she wanted, because if she did, then she would be forced to come to terms with the fact that she hadn't a snowball's chance in hell of ever getting it.

Covering a sudden feeling of devastating loss, she said, "I'll just go and make myself a sandwich. Please don't feel that you have to entertain me. I—my notes . . . That is, perhaps you're right—an early night . . ."

Quint stood aside and bowed her toward the kitchen door. "Go get yourself whatever you want, honey. You'll feel better when you've had some supper. My mama always said food was a great peacemaker."

Her head lifted another degree. "Thank you."

"You feel like making another one while you're at it?"

"I believe one will be sufficient. I—oh. For you, you mean."

"Don't go to any extra trouble."

If there'd been a size-six hole in the floor, she'd have crawled into it. "It's no trouble."

"You're sure? Then that'd be right nice." His smile was not only sincere, it was all out of proportion to what she'd so grudgingly offered, and Chloe suddenly felt ashamed. Just because her own nerves were on edge, she didn't have to take it out on the rest of the world.

"There's only cheese and butter," she warned him, sounding shrewish, but unable to help herself. "You shouldn't go so heavy on high-fat, high-cholesterol foods at your age."

Quint arched his brows in surprise. "Well, I reckon at my age, there's a lot of stuff I ought to pass up. For one thing, I'm getting too damned old to put up with so much sexual frustration." She gasped, but he went right on. "On the other hand, I reckon I'm also too old to—uh . . ." For the first time, he seemed to grow aware of the dead-end alley he'd backed himself into.

She could only stare at him. "I beg your pardon?" she managed finally.

Quint was still floundering around in an effort to extricate his big foot when Chloe made her escape. "Sandwiches," she muttered, and dashed for the security of the kitchen, her cheeks burning as they hadn't burned since she was twelve years old and had got her first period at a birthday party for the boy next door.

You're thirty-three years old, for heaven's sake! You're no blushing adolescent. Just because a man happens to kiss you in passing, you don't have to flop around gasping for air like a landed trout!

She ordered herself to march right back out there and ask if he wanted coffee, milk or iced tea to drink with his cheese sandwich, but before she even reached the swing door, she heard the front door open and close, and the sound of the pickup roaring off into the night.

To her great astonishment, and rather to Quint's, Chloe suspected, the routine they established over the next few days was quite comfortable. Since she'd learned there wasn't a hotel in town, nor a motel within walking distance of Buster's garage—and since they both knew the limited extent of her finances—no more was said about her leaving. Quint rose early each morning and made coffee, while Chloe, in spite of Urk's best efforts, remained in bed until after she'd heard him drive away.

She came to enjoy the soothing murmur of the pigeons as they waddled up to the house for the cracked corn Quint kept in a tin just inside the back door.

"You know a good thing when you find it, don't you, darlings?" she crooned, tossing out handfuls of the feed just to watch the lovely blue-and-lavender birds gobble it up. "I always knew there was some reason I liked pigeons—we have a lot in common, did you know that? We both know a good roost when we find one."

After breakfast, she would set about making plans for the day. Janet had assured her that she had neither the time nor the inclination to get involved in interior decoration, and after promising to send around a handyman to help clear away the accumulation of junk, she gave her the names and numbers of the firm's workmen, who were currently at liberty.

"I'm sure Quint will be glad to pay you for your efforts," she'd said, but when Chloe had protested that her room and board were payment enough, the woman had shrugged as if it mattered not one whit to her that her fiancé was living with a young, unattached woman.

But then, why should it bother her? Janet was the one holding up the wedding, not Quint. According to her, he'd been ready to dispense with the whole business of an engagement and get the job done by a justice of the peace.

"You're probably wondering why I'm not drifting around in a rosy haze, spouting a bunch of hearts-and-flowers nonsense," she'd said just the day before when she'd stopped by to collect some papers from Quint's wall safe. Chloe had just brewed herself a pot of tea and Janet had accepted her offer of a cup before she dashed off to Rocky Mount for another business meeting.

"No. Actually, I hadn't given it much thought," Chloe had demurred, mentally crossing her fingers.

"Quint was in love with my baby sister," Janet had stated bluntly. She'd been wearing khaki gabardine, which had done nothing at all for her coloring. Chloe remembered wishing she could take the other woman to her own hairdresser for a cut and a rinse, and perhaps a facial, and then have her try on something in a soft pastel.

"Marissa was the beauty of the family," Janet had said, and Chloe had started guiltily, wondering if she'd been completely transparent. "They were so crazy about each other it was embarrassing to be in the same room with them—but then Quint got sent to Vietnam.''

It was the first Chloe had known that Quint was a veteran, but it fit. That overgrown sense of responsibility of his would have made him get involved. ''What happened?'' she asked, before good sense and good manners could intervene.

Janet had shrugged. She'd lighted a cigarette and blown a stream of smoke across the room. ''Marissa was the baby, like I said. She was spoiled rotten—we all did it. I was as bad as the rest of them, and I was only seven years older than she was. The thing is, she's always been so beautiful it just wasn't possible not to give in to her. Whatever Rissa wanted, Rissa got. And naturally, she wanted Quint, because all the girls were nuts about him when he was growing up. Our families were in business together, so we all saw a lot of each other, but Quint had always looked on Rissa as a kid sister.''

She had stubbed out her cigarette and lighted another one, and Chloe had tried not to wrinkle her nose at the acrid smell of the overflowing ashtray. ''But then one day, Quint took a second look at little Rissa—I reckon she was all of seventeen or eighteen then—and he fell, hook, line and sinker. Lord, how he loved that girl! They got engaged before he went overseas, and he used to write to her all the time. She let me read the letters. They weren't the only ones she got from men, you understand. Like I said, Rissa was beautiful. She had men swarming around her from the time she was fourteen.''

Chloe's hands had come up defensively. She'd known in advance that some tragedy must have occurred. Poor Marissa had been killed in an accident. She had died of some awful disease before Quint could get to her.

"The trouble was, Rissa had never learned patience. All she had to do was snap her fingers, and whatever she wanted was hers. So when Elliott came driving up in his new Corvette after Quint had been gone for nearly a year, one look was all it took. Poor Rissa had had enough of staying home while all the other girls were out having fun, so she started going out with him."

She'd sighed and Chloe had felt a stirring of sympathy for the older, plainer sister of Marissa Bond. "It's understandable," she'd murmured. "Your sister couldn't have been very old."

"Nineteen by then—nearly twenty—but still the baby. I reckon we didn't do her any good, indulging her the way we did, giving her everything she wanted— letting her get away with murder." Janet had nodded her head, causing her short straight hair to swing against her cheeks.

Poor Marissa. Poor Quint. Poor Janet.

But then Chloe had never, even at her most miserable, been egotistical enough to believe that she was the only woman in the world whose life had unexpectedly collapsed around her head. "So did she—?"

"Dump him? You got it."

"Poor Quint," Chloe had said, and Janet had looked surprised.

"Poor Elliott is more like it—the little devil took him for everything he had, and now she's off with number three. At least there weren't any children. Thank God for that.''

In spite of years of training, Chloe hadn't been able to come up with a single diplomatic response. She needn't have worried. Once she'd begun, Janet had seemed determined to hang out the entire family laundry for all to see.

''I think that's the closest Daddy and Jethro Stevens ever came to breaking up the partnership. I do remember that Camilla, Quint's mother, hardly spoke to Mama for years after that, and with them belonging to the same church circle and all, things got pretty uncomfortable.''

For a long time, neither of them had said anything more. Then Janet had got up and crossed the room to a wall safe that had been hidden behind the china cabinet in the dining room. ''This junk has got to come out of here—oops! Caught 'em!''

After placing the stack of soup plates on the cluttered table, she'd opened the wall safe, removed a thick envelope and shut the door again, twirling the dials.

Chloe had watched her silently as Janet glanced quickly over the papers. Not until Janet had glanced up again did Chloe speak. ''You know, you're awfully trusting.''

''Who, me? Oh—you mean the safe. Sorry to disappoint you, but there's not a thing in there that would do you any good. Take my word for it.''

It hadn't been the safe Chloe had been talking about, but before she could find a graceful way of putting it, the older woman had grinned and said, ''If you're talking about Quint, then you can relax. Quint and I understand each other.''

For an intelligent woman, Janet struck her as remarkably dense at times. Or perhaps it was Chloe who was dense. It wouldn't be the first time she'd misread a situation and come up the loser. "I'm glad to hear it," she'd responded faintly.

Perching on the dangerously overloaded table, Janet had crossed a pair of neat ankles and begun to swing her muddy, low-heeled pumps. "Look, Chloe, we all know that for some reason, you seem to be down on your luck. If I had to risk a guess, I'd say you were newly divorced. But it's none of my business, and I don't even want to know. I do know you're smart enough to take advantage of the present situation, but hell—I might even do the same thing in your place." Her voice had held no malice, but it had held no warmth, either.

Chloe, feeling suddenly chilled, had clasped her arms in front of her, her gaze never wavering.

"Just don't get to feeling too comfortable here, huh? And don't underestimate me. I'm too smart to get Quint's protective instincts all worked up by kicking you out on your pretty little behind, but don't push me. And don't—I repeat, do *not*—dig in too deeply."

Chloe had felt as if someone had knocked the breath out of her; but gamely, she'd bobbed back up again. "I'm not intruding on your territory, Janet. And while I'm not saying the idea hasn't crossed my mind, it would never work. You don't know me, so I don't expect you to take my word for anything. But don't sell Quint short. He has far more integrity than you give him credit for."

"Maybe. Maybe not. Quint's a man, and like most men, he'll take what's offered. But don't fool your-self—there's nothing here for you. Oh, he's okay, but he's not in your class either socially or financially. Not all successful business owners graduate from a fancy Ivy League school, you know. Quint didn't graduate at all. He enlisted in his junior year at State, but even without a degree, he's still smart enough to know that women like you don't settle for guys like him—not for long."

By then Chloe had been too furious to speak, even if she'd had something to say. She was no snob, but even if she had been, Quinton Stevens was worth more than any other man she'd ever met. He and her late husband weren't even the same species!

Janet had gone on talking, and Chloe had pulled herself together in time to hear her say, "So sleep with him if you have to—go ahead and make use of his house and his money for as long as you need it. But remember this: I'll still be here long after you're gone. I'm not in your league when it comes to looks, but I've got something you haven't—something that means a hell of a lot more to Quint than a warm body and a pretty face. He learned a long time ago just how much those are worth."

"Janet, please—I'm sure you don't mean any of—"

"I might not be centerfold material, but I do hap-pen to own forty-nine percent of Quinton's business. And there's not one damned thing he can do about it, because I don't intend to sell, and he knows it. Once I get around to telling him to jump, he'll jump, all right. Don't you doubt it for one minute, honey. Meanwhile, I don't mind using you while you're here. This place could do with a little polish, and I'd as soon you whipped it into shape as pay one of those hotshot Raleigh decorators we keep on retainer. I figure a week should about do it, don't you? Meanwhile, if you need a loan to get you on your way, ask *me*—not Quint. If I read you right, you've got a damned sight too much pride to ask any man for money."

Chapter Eight

She was doing it again—creating. Working beside old Sonny Armbruster, the man Janet had sent to help clear the way for the painters, Chloe would find herself creating scenes and dialogue for a man and a woman who were obviously husband and wife, and just as obviously madly in love.

"Wait! Don't try to lift that box, Sonny, it's too heavy." *Wait—don't try to lift that box, honey, it's too heavy.* "No point in breaking your back over a heap of old magazines. Let's slide it through to the utility room for now."

"Yes'm. That ol' kitchen's gonna look some kinda nice, all done up, ain't it?"

"With a lot of scrubbing and a little paint—oops! Wait'll I brush these cobwebs out of my hair and I'll get the door for you, Sonny."

Candlelight flickered on the pale paneled walls, bringing dancing highlights to Chloe's golden hair. Abruptly, Quinton rose from his place at the head of the table and came around beside her, kneeling on the wide-plank floor...the Aubusson...the pale green Tabriz...

Oh, for heaven's sake, let Janet choose the floor coverings, Chloe fumed silently. She'd be the one to walk on them.

And on Quint. That thought came unbidden, and Chloe forced it from her mind. It was none of her business. She had spent the past three days working to repay Quint's hospitality, while he had caught up on the work he'd neglected, thanks to her inopportune visit. He left early each morning, stayed late each day, and as often as not, brought Janet home with him at night to check on the progress Chloe and Sonny had made.

In fact, Chloe seldom saw him anymore without Janet along. If she didn't know better, she might think that Janet was keeping an eye on her—or that Quint was using his fiancée as a buffer.

Ridiculous, she chided herself as she grabbed another carton of canning jars and slid them through to the utility room. Just because she happened to be thrown into his company for a few days—just because he happened to be the nicest man she'd met in ages—just because he happened to be the sexiest man she'd ever laid eyes on...

After pushing the carton to one side along with the others, Chloe lingered a moment, her gaze settling on one of Quint's old jackets that was tossed over the washer. How strange that she should think of him—or of any man—in that context. Her own sexuality had been in deep freeze for so long, she was shocked that she'd even noticed.

Sonny left at four, and Quint and Janet arrived just after dark. While Chloe showed them both the progress made that day, Janet continued to talk to Quint about business matters. Just as if they hadn't spent the entire day together, Chloe thought rancorously.

As soon as possible, she excused herself on the pretext of a headache. If Janet was deliberately trying to shut her out, she was succeeding.

With each passing day Quint grew more aloof. It was as if those brief moments of tenderness—the laughter over Urk's antics and the sharing of long, quiet hours while they each read—or pretended to read—were forgotten.

As for the kisses they had shared, Chloe ardently wished they had never happened. She was pretty certain Quint was regretting them, too. He had taken to staring at her when he thought she wasn't watching, and looking away the instant she met his gaze. He seldom offered her so much as a smile anymore, let alone the easygoing companionship she'd come to enjoy so much during her first few days as his guest.

At least she'd found a niche, as unlikely as it was, where she could bide her time and make plans for the future. She was sleeping well and thinking much more clearly—completely unlike the nervous creature who had fled Florida with no clear idea what she was running toward, only what she was leaving behind. In fact, if she'd deliberately set out to find an environment that was the complete opposite of the one she'd left, she couldn't have done a better job of it.

There was only one problem, and that one was so absurd as to be laughable. A side effect, that's all it was—a perfectly natural side effect, brought on by being thrown into close proximity with a man like Quinton Stevens....

"You need help stackin' them boxes, Miz Chloe?"

"Oh, Sonny! You startled me. I think what we really need is a small herd of trained elephants. Or maybe goats. Did Quint's mother really plan to re-read all these old magazines?"

"No'm, I reckon not. But some folks don't throw away what was hard to come by. Reckon Miz C'milla figgered she'd find a use for them old papers one day, only the day never come."

"Remind me not to store up piles of junk for some-one else to have to dispose of, will you?" Chloe mur-mured absently.

"Yes'm, I'll do that. Now you just go set down in the front parlor a spell an' leave me to look after this mess."

Chloe laughed aloud. "Believe it or not, that's about all I've done for the past thirty-three years. I've just discovered that I like getting my hands dirty and my muscles involved. Can you believe the progress we made today?"

"Ain't gonna be no progress if you get your back all ruint. Now you take Miz Jessica—that's Miss Janet's mama. That ol' lady don't care nothin' for nobody's back, long's it ain't hers."

Having long since accustomed herself to Sonny's double and triple negatives, Chloe only smiled in commiseration. "Miz Jessica" was not one of old Sonny's favorite people; that much was clear.

"Leastwise, I won't be hauling trash for Miss Janet, cause that woman don't let nothing pile up under her feet. Somepin' outlive its use, and she jus' throw it out, and tha's a fact!"

Chloe straightened her own protesting back and brushed her hair away from her face. "Look how low the sun's getting. Why don't we quit for the day and have a cup of coffee? I think there're still a few doughnuts from the box Quint brought home yesterday."

Sonny's hours were limited to between ten and four, three days a week, so as not to jeopardize his Social Security. That suited Chloe just fine. On the off chance that Quint should happen to come home early for once, she'd hate like the dickens to be caught looking like last year's scarecrow in one of his old shirts, a pair of filthy white slacks, her single braid dull with dust and cobwebs, and a pair of his thick slipper socks tied around her ankles with the ribbons from her peignoir.

Over coffee, Sonny would regale her with tales of growing up in Gumtree Corners, logging the swamps for cypress, setting rabbit traps, stewing the meat and selling the pelts, and hunting black bear with Jethro Stevens and a much younger Quint.

Today he told her about his wine making. "I uses them little black grapes that grows in the swamp, and pears off'n my own tree, and roses out'n Miz Jessica's garden. Them roses is what gives it such a fine taste," Sonny swore. "I get 'em when the moon dew's still wet on 'em."

In other words, Chloe thought with amusement, he stole them in the dead of night. She smiled and, encouraged, he went on. "It come to me once when I was cuttin' Miz Jessy's grass, and I heard some of her high-steppin' lady friends goin' on about rosie wine and bouquets, and I been making it that way ever since. I'll bring you a jug tomorrow. I just put it up last month, so it's still fresh."

Chloe said she could hardly wait, and saw the bent old man off toward his own home, which was less than a mile down a logging road through the forest.

Inhaling the hint of wood smoke in the crisp air appreciatively, she turned away, her mind on the deep, hot soak in the tub she intended to have. But before she'd even reached the door, she heard Quint's car pull up in the driveway.

Of all the rotten luck! Today of all days, when she'd worn the same makeshift costume to work in all week, he would choose to come home early.

"I passed your sidekick on the way out," Quint called as he strode up the leaf-covered front walk. He was alone today. "You two aren't overdoing things, are you? There's no rush, you know."

Chloe mumbled something and slipped inside the door, hoping to escape. With a business meeting in Plymouth today, Quint had left half an hour later than usual, wearing a dark gray pin-striped suit, a pearl-gray shirt and a maroon Paisley tie. He'd looked stunning at seven forty-five in the morning. Even half asleep, she'd been badly shaken by the swift rush of longing that had swept over her as she'd watched him drive away.

Now, dammit, he was more stunning than ever, despite his open collar, his twisted necktie, the thick hair that had suffered from his fingers raking through it, and the shadow that darkened his stubborn jaw.

Feeling like a swimmer going down for the third time, Chloe willed herself to be somewhere else. By the time Quint reached the front door, she was halfway up the stairs, her progress sorely hampered by the flapping slipper-socks.

"Whoa there! What the hell is that on your feet?"

Cornered, she turned and attacked. "They're called slipper socks! If I had a pair of flat shoes with the toes and heels in, do you think I'd be wearing these—these *things*?" she snapped, glaring first at him and then at her feet. "Don't worry—the tag inside says they're washable, and I seriously doubt if I stretched them out of shape!"

He started up the stairs after her. "I'll see if Janet has something you can—"

"Don't you dare! I'm not in the habit of borrowing personal items!" She felt for the step behind her and took it.

From his vantage point below her, Quint gazed sharply at the drooping navy flannel shirt with the rolled-up sleeves, the outsize slipper socks tied with neat satin bows, and the pair of slacks that were obviously expensive and had probably once been white. She looked like a clown. A beautiful, lovable, furious, homemade clown. "Yeah. Right. You're not going to believe this, honey, but I happen to own a shirt and a pair of slipper socks exactly like yours." He took three steps forward, and she backed up two. "How's that for a coincidence, hmm?"

"Don't be absurd. You know what I meant."

"Uh-huh," he purred again. He was no more than three steps below her by then, which put their eyes on a level. And his were laughing.

"Naturally I'll have your things laundered before I go." Damn, she needed a bath in the worst kind of way! She absolutely *hated* to be seen like this—by anyone, but particularly by Quinton Stevens. Especially when he was looking like the cover of one of the better men's magazines, and smelling of wool and soap and cold November air.

"Naturally," he agreed, stalking her one more step. She hastily felt with her left foot for the step above, one hand clutching the golden oak banister, the other one trailing gray finger-marks up the pale green wallpaper.

"Listen, why don't you go downstairs and look into your old kitchen—you're going to be amazed at how much we've accomplished today...."

He was grinning openly now, and Chloe felt like taking a swing at him. She had never been physically aggressive—certainly she'd never struck another human being, although there'd been a few times...
"I—uh—I just thought I'd take a bath before I start on dinner," she explained hurriedly, not taking her eyes from his.

She was filthy. Not only that, she probably *smelled* filthy! Her father had once thrown a royal fit when she'd spilled tomato bisque on her dress at dinner. He'd called her a mannerless young heathen in front of eight dinner guests and sent her to eat the rest of her meal alone in her room. She'd been fourteen at the time, and so proud of being included in a grown-up dinner party.

As for Brice, he hadn't even been able to bear seeing her without her makeup.

Stop it! You're an adult—if you want to spill your soup, then you can damn well spill your soup!

Glaring down at Quint, she started to tell him so, when he swooped and caught her before she could jump out of the way. "Would you puh-*lease*—!" she squawked.

"Quiet. Any woman who'd back up a slippery staircase in her sock feet needs all the help she can get." His arms locked into place around her back and under her thighs, and he carried her the rest of the way to the bathroom and shouldered open the door.

"I wouldn't have been backing up if you hadn't—"

"But you were. Now, get out of that rig and into a hot tub, and I'll see about fixing something to eat. Janet's coming over later, and I'd like us to be finished when she gets here."

Not until he lowered her onto the tile floor and shut the door behind him did Chloe breathe freely again. She was shaking with anger—and something else that didn't bear close scrutiny—by the time she had untied her ribbons and stripped off her filthy clothes.

Her slacks were ruined. Even her bra was soiled from all the dirt that had fallen down her neck as she lifted down dozens of empty canning jars from a high shelf in the old kitchen.

Turning on both faucets full blast, she found herself wishing Quint could have had a flat tire on the way home from Plymouth. Better yet, four flats. Maybe then he wouldn't have strolled in looking so smug.

She was going to have to leave immediately—car or no car. And while she hated to leave a job half done, there was more at stake here than interior decoration. Her sanity, for instance.

She'd thought she could do what was needed, remaining uninvolved, and then, when the job was done or her car was finished, and sold, whichever came first, she could be on her way, sane and sound and ready to get on with her life. That wasn't a whole lot to ask, was it?

As the daughter of a socially prominent banker and the wife of an ambitious young politician, Chloe had grown quite adept at fitting herself into her surroundings, at organizing, and at getting along with strangers without ever becoming personally involved.

Only something was going wrong here. The more she did to prepare Quint's home for its new mistress, the more involved she became. It was bad enough to fall in love with a house, but that wasn't the worst of it.

She had to get out of here. That's all there was to it. It just wasn't working out. She was already coveting the house, with all its quirks and peculiarities, with its massive oaks and tall pines, its resident rooster and flock of lovely homing pigeons. But far worse, she was beginning to covet its owner. And that could only cause problems. In the first place, he was a man; and in her experience, men were not to be trusted. And even if by some fluke he returned her feelings, there was Janet. Which would make Chloe no better than that redhead from Georgia, Sheila Warden, who had ruined the small chance of happiness she could have had with Brice.

* * *

"You'd better take it easy today," Quint said the following morning. He was back to his usual corduroys worn with a turtleneck sweater, and it was all Chloe could do to keep her hands off him, much less her eyes.

Feigning a calmness she was far from feeling, she poured herself a cup of coffee and leaned against the sink to watch the few pigeons come out of the loft. "I should think they'd want to find another flock, or colony, or whatever one calls bunches of pigeons, and start a new family. Don't they get lonely?"

"Hmm? Oh, the homers, you mean." He slathered butter on two slices of bread and layered them with slabs of Cheddar. "These guys mate for life. There's probably a mixture of males and females in the flock—I can't tell 'em apart. But if there're not the right males with the right females, and vice versa, then that's it. No eggs, end of story."

"Do they always come back here?"

Quint nodded. "Dad used to race them. He'd take 'em as much as five hundred miles away and release them, and they'd invariably beat him home. I don't do anything but feed them nowadays, but I enjoy having them around."

"They're lovely," murmured Chloe, a bit skeptical over the tale of so much fidelity. But perhaps birds knew something men didn't.

"Like I said, you'd better take it easy today. Wouldn't want you to have a relapse." He bit into his cheese sandwich, and Chloe wondered how long it had been since someone had cooked him a real breakfast.

She didn't dare offer. Things were tough enough as it was.

"Sonny and I are almost done. I'd like to leave everything ready for the cleaners and painters, and one more day will do it."

"Then make it tomorrow," he said curtly.

She stiffened. "Tomorrow I intend to be on my way north."

"Your car's not finished."

"Buster and I have an understanding." From the latest of their daily phone conferences, Chloe understood she was being taken to the cleaners, and Buster understood he had a sucker right where he wanted her. But it was the best she could do, and it would have to serve.

"You can understand each other just as well a few days from now. You're not ready to move on."

"Quint, I've already been here nearly two weeks."

"So? I wasn't aware you were rushing to keep an appointment."

"Which reminds me," she interjected, "I owe you for several long-distance calls."

"Forget it," he answered gruffly. And then, as though he couldn't help himself, he asked if she'd been in touch with her family.

Chloe sighed and twisted the warm mug in her hands. She had told him little about her plans. She didn't particularly want to talk about her family. "I've tried to call my cousin in Maryland, but I keep getting her answering machine—which means you get charged for completed calls—and I still haven't a clue where she is. I hate machines."

"This cousin—she's the one you were on your way to visit?"

"Mmm-hmm."

"What's she like?"

"Ginny? Oh, she's very reliable. Everybody says Ginny got all the common sense in the family." That should set his mind to rest. With that overgrown sense of responsibility of his, there was no telling what he might do if she told him the truth—that the cousin she had counted on was evidently off on vacation, or on one of her sudden, unexplained jaunts.

The woman turned up the collar of her trench coat and stepped into the light. It was Virginia. And that piece of cold steel she was clutching was leveled right at his heart.

Quint wasn't satisfied with the answers he'd been getting. That alone was enough to make him uneasy. And *that* made him mad!

Let her leave, he fumed to himself. It was no skin off his nose. He'd only brought her here in the first place because he didn't have the heart to dump her.

Let her go! She was back on her feet, looking a damned sight better than she had when he'd hauled her out of her car. She was of age, of sound mind, and if she wanted to go, he'd let her go—he didn't have a problem with that.

Yeah. The only thing he had a problem with was keeping his mind on his work and his hands in his pockets. And that was *definitely* a problem! The sooner she got on her way, the sooner he could settle back into his comfortable rut and get on with his life.

He grunted. That idea was about as appealing as wet bread. The trouble was, he was beginning to feel trapped. And restless. And moody as hell. Quint thought he'd got over being moody a long time ago. It had taken him a good whack of time to work the war out of his system—less to work through Marissa's defection. Still, he'd managed to get through both love and war a long time ago, and he'd been on an even keel ever since.

Until now.

Spinning his worn leather chair around, Quint propped his feet on the windowsill and gazed out over the random assortment of cars and trucks in the parking lot of Stevens-Bond Development, Inc. As much as he hated to admit it, his home had taken on a whole different feeling since Chloe Palmer had moved in. He found himself hating to leave for work in the mornings and anxious to rush right home in the evenings. And under the circumstances, that was a problem.

Janet stuck her head in his door. "Hixton's in my office about those estimates we promised him by Friday. You want to talk to him about the berm first? Zoning approved the variance, but it's going to cost us like the devil."

Estimates. The berm. "Oh, yeah—sure. I'll be along in a minute. Say, Janet, you want to come for dinner tonight?"

"Again?" Her thick brown hair swung as she shook her head. "What the hell is going on, Quint—you trying to court me or something?"

"Try the 'or something,'" he said with a rather halfhearted laugh.

* * *

Chloe was frowning even before she put down the phone. Dinner for four? Things were getting entirely too cozy when Quint—or Janet, whichever one was responsible—started bringing along an extra man for her. The three of them had managed well enough all week long, with Chloe tactfully finding something to do in her room as soon as the dishes were cleared away.

"This is the last time," she vowed as she went out to the utility room to survey the contents of the freezer. Tomorrow she was going to quit trying to coerce Buster into a more favorable deal and take the old clunker and the three thousand dollars he'd offered. Her car was worth at least twenty, and even with the repairs, three was an insult.

Unfortunately she was in no position to quibble.

At six-thirty, Chloe came back downstairs, sniffing the enticing aroma of roast chicken and scalloped potatoes. She'd driven Quint's car into Williamston to shop for groceries and stopped by the garage for one more attempt to talk Buster out of a few thousand more dollars.

Three thousand and a drivable vehicle—never mind that it had visible rust and ninety-seven thousand miles on the odometer. That was his final offer, take it or leave it.

She'd muttered obscure threats under her breath all the way home, for all the good it had done. Women and cars and mechanics were a losing combination, but there was no way she was going to bring Quint in on it!

* * *

"About time," Quint observed, looking around at the sound of the squeaking front door. Chloe made a mental note to ask Sonny to oil the hinges. "Hey, did I screw up? I thought we'd agreed on informal."

"We agreed on dinner, that's all." With her eyes riveted on the stunning portrait of rough masculinity he presented, Chloe was at first hardly even aware of the two others entering the room.

Janet looked as if she'd come directly from work. She was wearing an oatmeal tweed suit, this time with a pink blouse that made her look more sallow than ever. She held a sheaf of papers in one hand.

It was Quint who made the introductions. "Chloe, John Adamson. John, this is my guest, Mrs. Palmer. She's responsible for whatever it is that's got my appetite in an uproar."

And then, to Chloe's astonishment, he turned brick red. "Hungry. Skipped lunch," he muttered, and opened the refrigerator to disappear behind the door.

Chloe came the few steps necessary to extend her hand to John Adamson, who was an insignificant-looking man except for a remarkably sweet smile. He looked rather like an elderly child in his rumpled flannels and tweed jacket.

"Mighty pleased, Miz Palmer." His voice was as soft as his smile, the East Carolina drawl more pronounced than in either of the others. "You up from Flor'da, they tell me."

"That's right. I hope you like chicken, Mr. Adamson. It's one of the few things I do with any degree of success." She'd put on a pair of ivory silk lounging pajamas with a brocaded jacket for warmth. Her hair was freshly washed and coiled on top of her head in its usual style, and she wore gold sandals with high heels in a conscious effort to bring her closer to Quint's level.

Quint, on the other hand, was wearing his usual corduroy jeans, the worn seams delineating his masculinity in a way that a three-piece suit never could. His black turtleneck shirt clung to a chest the approximate size of a bushel basket, and Chloe felt her palms grow damp. Years of hard-earned poise deserted her and she leaped on the first topic that came to mind. "Quint, I forgot to ask—would you like to keep the jars?"

He pulled his head out of the refrigerator, his color back to normal. "Would I like to *what*?"

"Jars. Dozens of them. Hundreds of them, all sizes. There were lids on a few, but they're all filthy. I set them out on the back porch—I didn't know what else to do."

"Screw the jars," Quint replied, and Chloe fiddled furiously with the knotted golden cords at her waist.

"Yes, well . . . at least that might have kept out the insects."

He began to chuckle, and after several seconds, Chloe smiled. And then she began to laugh. Neither of them was even conscious that the other pair was staring at them in open amazement.

"Look, while you two fruitcakes dish up supper, why don't I go show Johnny the figures you came up with today, Quint. You did bring them home with you, didn't you?"

"Hmm? Oh, the figures? Yeah, sure—look on the dining-room table."

Desperately needing activity, Chloe began shaking the jar in which she'd mixed her salad dressing. "I hope you like garlic," she said after the other two had left.

"My favorite vegetable. Which plates do you want to use? Real ones or plastic?"

"Oh, real ones, by all means. I didn't think to ask if the others like garlic—I'm afraid I just went ahead and made it the way I like it."

"No problem. If they don't like it, they can use oil and vinegar."

For reasons that escaped her, Chloe felt compelled to bring Janet into the conversation again and again. "Does—that is, did Janet mind bringing Mr. Adamson along?"

Counting out the forks, which Chloe had polished just that morning, Quint looked up and said, "She was planning to go out with him tonight anyway, so I invited the two of them here instead. I think she's trying to get him feeding out of the palm of her hand before she reels him in."

Tearing lettuce leaves, Chloe searched the words for a sign of jealousy and found none. "I've heard of mixed metaphors, but that one stands alone."

Coming up beside her to sniff at the chicken she'd just removed from the oven, Quint remarked, "That's all you know, woman. I could show you a pond where the crappie come right up and eat bread from your fingers."

"Surely you wouldn't have the heart to hook a fish who'd eaten from your fingers."

"Why not? Bait's bait, any way you present it."

They were still bantering when the other two joined them. Janet took her place at the foot of the long pine table, with Quint at the head. It was the logical arrangement, yet Chloe found herself resenting it.

Oh, yes, it was long past time she left. She was developing a nasty little streak of possessiveness that would spell trouble if it wasn't nipped in the bud.

"When are you leaving, Chloe?" Janet asked, as if reading her thoughts.

"Tomorrow," Chloe replied at the same time Quint said, "Maybe in a week or so."

Janet looked from one to the other, while John busied himself with the chicken and baked vegetables.

"I saw Buster again today. We've come to a final agreement, so there's no reason for me to stay on."

"I'm sure you'll be glad to get on to wherever it is you're headed," Janet stated briskly.

"I think Doc McCall wants to give you a once-over before you take off," Quint put in, which Chloe didn't believe for one minute.

Over coffee—Chloe's version, not Quint's—they discussed the weather, the tobacco market, the price of copper and the alarming rate at which local cypress was being exported to Japan. At a lull in the conversation, Chloe excused herself, saying she needed to begin packing.

"I reckon you pretty well spread yourself out all over the place, didn't you?" Janet asked, and for the first time, Chloe felt active dislike for the other woman.

"Not really," she replied quietly. "I tend to be fairly organized, so it won't take me long to get everything together. And since I probably won't see you again before I leave, Janet, I'll say goodbye now. It's been—nice knowing you." The pause was purely unintentional, and she could only hope no one had noticed. She bade John Adamson good-night and goodbye, and managed to say something appropriate to Quint. She didn't dare look at him—for fear of what her eyes might reveal.

It was barely an hour later when Chloe heard Quint coming upstairs. She glanced quickly at her door to be sure it was closed, and went on with her packing. She'd changed into her gown and peignoir, leaving out only her beige slacks and sweater to wear tomorrow.

She hoped her new car had an efficient heater, or she might end up shopping before she ever left Williamston.

"Chloe? Are you still awake?" Without waiting to be invited in, Quint opened the door.

"I meant what I said about your not leaving so soon," he began, his dark eyes taking in the neatly packed suitcases and the outfit she'd folded over the rocker.

"And I meant what *I* said," she replied, folding the clothes she had just removed and placing them in a plastic bag to drop off at a cleaner's once she got settled.

He came into the room and she felt cornered. She moved toward the windows, needing air—needing space—and he followed her there. "Don't leave, Chloe. Not yet."

Panic began to prickle inside her, and she moved again, putting the rocking chair between them. "It's time, Quint. I'm healed, I have transportation, and I've done all I can for your house—for you and Janet. There's no more reason for me to stay."

"There is a reason," he insisted.

Wordlessly, she stared at him.

"There's a damned good reason, only I can't put it into words. Not yet. Just trust me, will you? Don't run away—give me a week."

"Quint, we both know I need to leave. It's not fair to Janet. She's been more than understanding about—"

"Understanding, hell! Look, I'm in no position to say anything now, but promise me you won't leave until I get some things straightened out. Promise me?"

Lord, but she was tempted! She had never been more tempted in her life, but there were too many reasons why she couldn't stay. "Why should I?" she asked, daring him to put it into words.

He was beside her in an instant, lacing his fingers through her neatly brushed hair. "Do I really have to tell you?"

"Quint, we're strangers. You don't even know me," she said a little desperately.

"I know enough. Some things are better known on a gut level. Reason just gets in the way."

Feeling her resolve begin to erode, Chloe tried to turn away, but he held her fast, his thumb and forefinger clamping her chin to tilt her face to his. "Chloe, please—"

"Would you let go of my chin? You're hurting me," she whispered.

"Tell me where I hurt you, let me kiss it."

She groaned, and then, as his face blocked out the overhead light, she panicked. Her mouth was open to protest the unfairness of what he was doing when his mouth came down over hers, and then all thought of resistance vanished like fog under a hot sun. Just as she'd feared, she melted the instant he touched her.

All the incredible feelings she'd almost convinced herself she had imagined the last time he'd kissed her were back, and with them a hundred more. Clinging to him, Chloe felt the heat racing through her veins like a sudden fever, and she knew it had been hopeless to believe she could escape unscathed. She'd been lost from the time he had first lifted her into his arms beside her ruined car and taken control of her life.

"No, please—you mustn't."

At her protest, he raised his head just enough to brush a dozen quick, sweet kisses on her cheek, her chin and her eyelids. "I know, I know." Once more he found her lips and traced the curving line between them with his tongue. "I keep telling myself that, but I don't believe it, and neither do you."

Unable to help herself, Chloe lifted her face again and captured his mouth with hers. Quint groaned deep in his throat, catching her in a crushing embrace as his body hardened like tempered steel in the flames that spread through them both.

"Lord, woman, what have you—" Without finishing, he caught her mouth again, kissing her more passionately than she had ever been kissed in all her thirty-three years.

"This just won't—"

"Don't say it," he whispered, holding her face into the curve of his throat.

Chloe inhaled the intoxicating essence of him, thrilling to a new element: one born of the two of them together. "Quint, I can't stay here after this," she said so softly she wasn't sure he had heard.

"I know, love, but you can't leave, either." His hands traced the too-slender lines of her back, sliding the silken garment over her skin. When his fingers trailed up her nape and tunneled through her hair, she tried to push him away.

"This isn't helping—it isn't right—it's not fair to—"

"Shh, let me take care of that," Quint interrupted. He allowed her to step back, but refused to release her completely. They were both breathing hard, their faces equally flushed. Chloe's wore the mark of Quint's late-day beard, for he never shaved a second time, even when he was going to be with Janet.

"Look, if I don't get out of here, I'm going to have you in that bed before either of us knows what's happening," he said in a rough whisper. "There are things I have to do first, so I'd better say good-night while I still can."

He paused at the door and looked back, and afterward, Chloe thought she would never forget the way he appeared at that moment. If she'd dared to believe the look in his eyes, she might have changed her mind about going.

But there was too much at risk. Janet deserved more. Quint deserved more.

And so did she. She had survived Brice's defection, the shameful end to her father's career, and his suicide. From now on, her life was going to be as risk free as she could possibly make it, and that meant no involvements. Especially no involvements with men who were already engaged to other women.

Chapter Nine

It was a conspiracy, Chloe decided. First the deluge, then the call from Buster, and then the dog. Especially the dog.

She had just hung up the phone after hearing from the garageman that her new-old car was going to have to be inspected before she could take it out on the highway, and that he couldn't get it done before noon, when Quint drove up and practically scraped the paint off the porch railing with his pickup truck.

She watched as he gathered something that looked like a bundle of filthy rags into his arms and dashed toward the door. Just before he got there, she opened it and stood back.

"Let's get this fellow into the house and see what ails him."

The bundle had begun to squirm the moment they reached the foyer, and Chloe, with one eye on Quint's muddy footprints and the other on the dubious "fellow" he was carrying in his arms, led the way to the utility room. She had a feeling all the cleanliness and orderliness she had achieved was about to come undone.

"Okay, old buddy. Nobody's gonna hurt you, just take it easy."

Standing uncertainly beside the door, Chloe listened as Quint crooned to the pathetic animal he'd brought home, and thought of Janet's derisive statement that he was always dragging home strays.

"Is he hurt?" she asked, tentatively moving closer.

"I don't know. I saw him lying beside the road about two miles back and stopped to investigate. He doesn't appear to be bleeding. No obvious breaks as far as I can see."

"But it's pouring rain," Chloe protested, kneeling beside him to peer at the filthy, nondescript dog who was resting patiently while Quint carefully examined his limbs. "He looks half drowned, poor darling."

"It's obvious you've never seen a half-drowned dog. Your 'poor darling' is sure 'nough suffering from something, but I doubt if it's rain. At least, not entirely. Hunger, I'd say. Plus a full complement of parasites."

Chloe shuddered but, bracing herself, she reached out a hand to pet the sad-looking creature on the head. Quint's fingers came around her wrist and he drew her hand back and tucked it into his lap.

"Don't you know any better than to try to touch a strange dog? He could take your hand off in one crunch."

"Unless his teeth are in as bad shape as the rest of him." She did her best to ignore the hand that was dangling across his thigh as the two of them squatted beside the dog. "I was only going to pat him on the head."

"He might not know that. Could be he's as stupid as he is ugly."

Chloe snatched her hand from its dangerous proximity to Quint's body and glared at him. "You don't have to be so insulting!"

He looked at her then for the first time, taking in her immaculate beige pants outfit, her neatly coiled hair and her carefully made-up face. "What the hell are you all gussied up for? Were you expecting company?"

Rising abruptly, Chloe stepped back to lean against the washer. That she'd managed to master the intricacies of the machine was a source of great pride, not that she would ever let him know that. "I was expecting Buster's helper to pick me up at nine in my new car." She had just begun to elaborate when Quint exploded.

With the dog cowering and shivering, he stood to deliver a blistering attack on ill-mannered, ungrateful women who sneaked out the minute one's back was turned without so much as a by-your-leave.

As if she needed his permission. "Are you quite finished?" she asked with icy politeness.

"When I'm finished, you'll damned well know it! Now go get into something practical and come help me with this—this *poor darling*!"

"You seem to be doing quite well without my help, and for your information I don't *own* anything practical!"

"That's the damned truth," he muttered under his breath. They were both standing by now, and Quint's eyes were drilling right through her brittle defenses. Chloe stubbornly glared right back at him, wishing she didn't feel so threatened by the sheer force of his masculinity.

A soft whine deflected their attention and they both turned to see the trembling dog rise shakily up on all fours. With a gentle cry, Chloe dropped down beside him and gathered him in her arms, completely disregarding both Quint's warning and her own costly silk sportswear.

"Poor darling, did he frighten you? He didn't mean it—some men are just unbearably surly, that's all."

"Surly, am I?" Quint knelt beside her, his hands ready to snatch the dog away from her at the first sign of trouble. "Women who don't have sense enough to look after themselves ought to appreciate a little well-meant advice."

"Advice!"

He scowled at her. "Yes, dammit. Advice! Now, put that animal down before you get yourself chewed up. In case you hadn't noticed, he's crawling with vermin."

"If you didn't want him, then why'd you bother to rescue him? This compulsion you have for dragging home strays is going to—"

"Oh, for crying out loud, what would you have done? Driven on by with your elegant little nose in the air? Yeah, you probably would, at that."

Chloe was livid. She couldn't remember the last time she'd been so furious. Another minute and she'd be screaming at him like a fishwife, and all over a wet, stinking, nondescript, homeless mutt.

If her father could have seen her now, he would have disowned her. Despite his own uncertain temper, H. Harrington Baskin could never abide what he termed a lack of breeding in the women around him.

"Oh—*bosh*!" Before she could disgrace herself further, Chloe relinquished the dog, spun on her heel and marched out of the room.

"Chloe!"

Fists clenched, she blinked rapidly to clear the tears from her eyes. Let him shout. She didn't need this. She didn't need *him*! What she needed was peace and tranquillity.

How deadly dull—nothing but peace and tranquillity!

"Chloe, dammit, you come back here!"

"Go take a flying leap, you big jerk!" she mumbled angrily as she stalked up the stairs. Seconds later, she slammed the bedroom door behind her and thumbed closed the small lever on top of the square metal lock mechanism. Whether the thing actually worked or not, it felt good to go through the motions of locking him out.

She was ticking off the minutes in the rocking chair when Quint flung open the door. So much for antique door latches. *Remember—peace and tranquillity. This jerk isn't worth the energy it takes to chew him out.*

"I didn't hear you knock," she said coolly.

"Quit trying to be cute. You know damned well I didn't knock. Why'd you run off like that?"

Chloe had the rocker up to thirty-seven miles an hour. She continued to stare determinedly out the window, her gray eyes dark as a thunderstorm. Not even the familiar scent of mothballs, lavender and lemon oil could soothe her now. "I had things to do up here."

"Yeah, so I see." His narrowed eyes took in the two suitcases on the painted iron bed. They were neatly packed, but not yet shut.

"You didn't need me to help with your dog."

Amid the flower-sprigged wallpaper, the embroidered-eyelet curtains and the other delicate furnishings of the old-fashioned bedroom, Quint looked strangely out of place—bigger, angrier, and more masculine than ever. "How do you know what I need and what I don't?" he demanded gruffly.

She had no answer for that. None that she dared offer, at any rate. "Is the dog all right?"

"Do you care?"

Her feet came down to the floor and stayed there. "Well, of course I care! Give me credit for that much, at least."

"Oh, I give you credit for a lot of things. For being a troublemaker, for being a—"

"Troublemaker!" She was astounded. Of all the charges he might have leveled against her, troublemaker was the most unexpected and undeserved. "I haven't the faintest idea what you're talking about."

"No? You think you can just walk into my house and—"

"I didn't walk, if you recall—I was carried!"

"It's all the same thing."

She rose from the chair and thrust out her chin at him, bracing her hips with her fists. "It is *not* the same thing! I didn't ask to come here. I didn't ask you to drag me away from my car. I didn't ask—" She broke off, eyes so full of angry tears that the man before her seemed to be swimming in space.

"Chloe?" His voice had lost all its steeliness now, and that made him all the more dangerous.

"Oh, forget it. I'm leaving the instant my car is delivered, and if you don't want your dog, I'll take the poor darling with me. I could do with some intelligent companionship for a change."

"No way, lady. Poor Darling stays here."

She drew a deep, shuddering breath and wondered if he took pleasure in deliberately tormenting her. She'd long since given up trying to understand the man—it would be easier to comprehend any one of the tons of civil-engineering tomes she had replaced in the newly cleared china cabinets.

Stress loads. She'd thumbed through the first one and come upon a chapter titled "Stress Loads." She should be an expert on those, by now.

"Find your own dog." There was a puzzling note of challenge in his voice that she declined to accept.

"Thanks, maybe I will. I might even stop by the local pound on the way out of town." Sure, she would—she couldn't even feed a goldfish, much less a dog.

"Good luck finding it."

Thoroughly dry-eyed by now, she shot him a hostile look, but he wasn't finished. "Look, Chloe, I didn't come up here to fight with you."

Her silky brown eyebrows arched skeptically. "No? You came to wish me bon voyage?"

"No, dammit. I thought—that is, maybe you could— Hey, look, do you think maybe we ought to call the vet?"

"The vet?" She felt for the back of the rocker and clutched the varnished canes. What sort of game was he playing now? "Don't ask me to make your decisions for you—I've never even owned a dog."

"Yeah, well...you're a woman. Women know things."

"All this woman knows is that you've dragged home another stray and your fiancée probably isn't going to be too thrilled, so if you want to avoid trouble you'll let me have the dog and I'll locate a vet on my way through town."

"Hold on there—Poor Darling is *my* dog. I found him, I'm keeping him."

Chloe shrugged. "You asked me."

"Forget it."

"Look, all I know is what you said, and—"

"Don't listen to what I say, dammit—listen to what I mean!" Desperately, Quint willed her to read his heart and give him a chance to make up for the botch he'd made of everything. He knew he wasn't particularly smooth, like the men she was used to. He hadn't even figured out what she was doing in his neck of the woods in the first place, but she was here, all right. And he'd been the one who found her.

And dammit, good looks and fashionable clothes and fancy city manners weren't everything! Sometimes a woman might need other things—such as the kind of steady caring that would last over the years, making the rough times bearable and the good times heaven on earth. And if it was that kind of caring she needed, then he could give it to her—all she would ever need, and then some.

But first he had to straighten out this mess with Janet. He should have known better than to go along with her on this marriage thing. It hadn't felt right but, the way she'd explained it, it had made sense—sort of. He hadn't particularly liked the notion of spending the rest of his life alone, and Janet felt the same way. How could he possibly have known that one week after he'd finally agreed to go through with it, an eight-point buck was going to turn his whole life upside down?

It came to him that either he had moved closer, or she had. They were standing no more than two feet apart by now. Not touching. Hardly even breathing.

"Quint, I—"

"Honey, you—"

"Smell like wet dog," Chloe finished. Unexpectedly a tremulous smile appeared on her lips, and suddenly they were both laughing. If Quint's eyes looked suspiciously damp, Chloe figured it was only because she was seeing him through her own tears. She stopped thinking altogether when his arms came around her and he drew her into the solid security of his powerful embrace.

"Thank God I saw that dog and came back. Were you really going to leave without even saying goodbye?" His lips moved against the heated curve of her neck, and she shuddered from the sensations that raced down her spine. They had come together like steel to a magnet. She didn't even know who had made the first move.

"I told you goodbye last night."

"Uh-uh. Last night was only a promise, love. I can't offer you much more than that, right now. But give me a few days—a week, at most. Will you do that?"

Chloe would have given him forever. She seemed to have lost all her scruples somewhere between yesterday and this wild, wonderful moment.

Poor Janet....

Then he was kissing her, and Janet and all the rest of the world disappeared. Heat built up quickly, and the scent of wet dog-hair mingled with French perfume, pine shampoo, sandalwood soap and the healthy, musky scent of Quint's skin.

The caress of his mustache sent a shower of exquisite sensations along her nerve endings as he nuzzled her throat. When she touched his cheek, he turned his face into her hand, and she felt the burning wetness of his tongue on her palm.

"I love the taste of you," he murmured.

She loved the taste of him, the feel of him, the touch of his hand on her breast. The air seemed suddenly too thin to sustain life, and she clung to him desperately when she felt his hard fingertips slide up under her sweater.

"Undress me," the woman cried as Mr. Y bent over her. "Please—I can't wait a moment longer!"

"I adore you. I was born to love you, and now I must have you—your beauty inflames me...."

"I promised myself I'd wait," Quint was saying, and Chloe laughed breathlessly. Then, somehow, they were on the bed. Afterward, she never remembered quite how they got there.

"Oh, please, I need—"

His mouth came down on hers, silencing her whispers. He knew what she needed, knew without her having to put it into words. And slowly, with a tenderness she could only wonder at, he gave it to her. While he kissed her, stroking her tongue with his, exploring, discovering, inflaming and promising, his hands were busy skimming her sweater up over her breasts. Without taking his mouth from hers, he began fumbling with the catch of her bra, and finally Chloe, fingers trembling, finished the job of unfastening it for him.

She heard the sound of a swiftly indrawn breath, and Quint said in a voice rough with feeling, "I knew you were lovely. I knew you'd look this way."

She was small and quite ordinary, but under the dark glow of Quint's gaze, she felt beautiful.

"Please?" she whispered unsteadily. The word was clearly an invitation, and he captured one small mound of her in his cupped hands and lowered his face to kiss the dusky nipple that had beaded to a peak long before the soft brush of his mustache even touched it.

He suckled her, paying equal attention to each breast. With her head thrown back, Chloe went quietly out of her mind. "You're so responsive," he murmured. "I never dreamed you would be so—"

"No, I—ahhhh. I can't stand it, Quint. I'm falling apart."

He had managed to unfasten the zipper at her side with far more deftness than he had shown with her bra hook, and one hand was easing the fabric down over her hips, his hard, hot hands smoothing over her skin until she thought she would scream from the tension.

"You, too," she said, reaching up to tug at his shirt. He was powerfully aroused. The visible evidence could have frightened her—instead, she found it wildly exciting. He was trembling, too, and that somehow made it all right.

"I want to feel your skin on mine." How bold she sounded! She had never in her life taken the lead in such matters, yet she wanted to tear off Quint's clothes and look her fill at his big, beautiful body, and then touch every inch of him, and kiss him in a way she had never dreamed of kissing any other man, not even her husband.

Insulated from the rest of the world by the steady drone of rain on the metal roof, they managed to get undressed, reveling in the touch and the taste of each other along the way. First Quint, and then Chloe, would lean away and look unabashedly, but then the wanting would take over and they would come together in a heated frenzy.

"I knew," he whispered roughly as he rolled on top of her to bury his face in her hair. "I knew the first time I ever saw you."

"Even then?" Her hands stroked his massive shoulders, toyed with the tufts of hair that made fascinating patterns in unexpected places on his body. Whatever happened was right. If she could do only one right thing in her life, let it be this!

"Even then," he murmured, letting her feel the full weight of him for one brief moment.

When he rose onto his knees, she pulled him back, her eyes opening in surprise.

"Quint? Sweetheart? What's wrong?"

Rolling onto his side, he drew her to him, holding her so tightly she could scarcely breathe. "Nothing's wrong, love. I just need a little more time, is all. You make me crazy, do you know that? I want you so bad I can't stand it, but—"

"But what?" She could feel herself shriveling into a small, protective ball. *Don't say it. I've heard it all before, and I refuse to hear it again!*

"Let's just lie here for a little while, all right? I doubt if I could walk if I tried." His arms were around her, her head pillowed on his shoulder so that her forehead was tucked up against his chin. For once, he was clean-shaven, she observed distractedly, and then she remembered that it was still morning.

Over the noise of the rain came the low, keening sound of the dog, and she stirred restlessly. The poor thing was probably feeling forsaken.

Dear Lord, could it feel any more forsaken than she did? Did Quint not want her, after all? No, she couldn't believe that. He'd said he wanted her; and anyway, some things were impossible to hide, and he'd—

And she had—

Oh, heavens, and then he had . . .

She had fallen apart in his hands. But then she had felt him begin to withdraw. It was as if a shadow had fallen over them—the shadow of Janet.

She had barely managed to pull herself together again when he said, "Do you hear what I hear?"

"I heard the dog. One of us had better go see about him, and since he's your dog . . ."

The phone rang, and Quint swore. "Oh, hell, I forgot all about the conference I scheduled for ten this morning."

"It might be for me," she said, but he was already extricating himself from their rather convoluted embrace. "How close to noon is it?"

If he answered her, she didn't hear. They were both making rather a production of getting dressed. "Must have kicked my other shoe all the way under the bed," Quint grumbled. Zipping his pants, he dropped down on all fours and reached for it.

Chloe could have cried. Either that or kicked him hard on the taut little behind he offered as a target.

She did neither; instead, she congratulated herself on having escaped a potentially messy business that would have ended up with at least one person getting hurt, and probably more.

Funny how empty self-congratulation could feel on a cold November morning three days away from Thanksgiving.

Chapter Ten

On the way to his offices outside Williamston, Quint dropped the dog off at a veterinarian's. He was going to be late anyhow—a few minutes more shouldn't matter. Before he'd left home he'd explained to Chloe about the meeting he'd finally succeeded in scheduling with the planning board about a variance in zoning he was trying to push through. He'd scheduled it the day after he'd met her. At that time, it had seemed vitally important.

Now, suddenly, the whole business seemed irrelevant. Only by reminding himself that if things worked out the way he was hoping, he couldn't afford to jeopardize important business contacts, was Quint able to keep from turning around and racing back home.

As soon as he settled the zoning matter, he was going to speak to Janet. It wasn't something he was looking forward to. After all, he worked with the woman six days a week. And regardless of what happened between them personally, he would still have a business association with her.

Why the devil had he allowed things to swing so far wide of center? He must have been crazy to go along with that harebrained scheme of hers to consolidate their professional relationship by getting married.

By the time he'd dropped the dog off and left instructions for the vet to give him the works, Quint was no nearer solving the problem of Janet. With his mind back home with Chloe, it was a wonder his body hadn't walked into a wall.

Grinning, he thought of the look the vet's receptionist had given him when he'd showed up at the office with the mutt.

"Name, please?"

"Uh—Poor Darling."

She'd waited a full thirty seconds before saying, "Okay, Mr. Darling, what's the dog's name?"

"Oh. That's his name. Mine's Quinton Stevens. Sorry."

"You don't have to apologize—I've heard worse," she'd said without even glancing up from the card she was filling out. "Breed?"

"Airedale and shepherd," he'd spouted off the top of his head. It was as good a guess as any.

Distracted, he ran a stop sign and drove two blocks past his turn. Who would have believed it possible for a dull, middle-aged backwoods contractor to fall so damned fast and so damned far?

On the way into his own office, he stuck his head in Janet's suite and spoke to her secretary. "She in yet?"

"Since eight. You need to see her? She's still on the phone."

"Never mind," Quint replied hastily. "Look, just keep her here, will you? I've got a meeting that'll last about—oh, twenty, thirty minutes, tops—and then I really need to see her. So nail her down for me, huh? Don't let her get away."

The secretary gave him a coy look that told him she'd misread the whole situation, which didn't help his disposition when he strode into his office to find the three gentlemen he'd invited there studying the project map on his west wall.

"Sorry I'm late, gentlemen. Shall we get right down to it?" With the same inherent air of authority that had earned him a field commission his first year in Nam, he indicated the leather visitors' chairs and took his own place in front of the window.

Chloe sniffled and resolved not to shed another tear as she left one more nameless town behind. The rain had cleared, leaving long furrows of reflected sky between rows of pale, broken cornstalks. She passed a small country fairground and felt every bit as forlorn as the tattered banners looked two days after the fair had ended.

It was cold. She should have gone shopping for suitable clothing instead of putting it off to some nebulous day in the future. What on earth had she been waiting for? A fairy godmother?

"Balderdash," she muttered, and forced herself to appreciate the sight of stark-white sea gulls wheeling over wet fields. She was going to miss being wakened every morning by a peanut-fed rooster and a bunch of mismatched homing pigeons.

A slash of sunlight broke through the dark clouds like a brilliant omen, and she told herself it was a sign of better things to come.

Better than what? What she'd known before? Or what she'd found when she'd tried to run away? She'd gone from a highly privileged and highly public life that had ended in disaster to the quietest, most comfortable kind of obscurity. From palm trees and limousines, country-club dances and private jets, to pine trees and pickup trucks, church suppers and pig pickings. As for private planes, the only one she'd seen around Gumtree Corners had been a crop duster.

Yet she'd felt such an affinity for the tiny farming and logging community. There was a somber richness about the land that was oddly reassuring. She would have given a lot to be able to see it in the summertime, with corn and cotton, tobacco and soybeans greening the fields for miles.

And Quint. He was like the land itself—deep, nourishing and solid; rich in ways she could never before have imagined. She'd spent almost two weeks living under his roof, learning to love a gaunt and cluttered old farmhouse with a resident assortment of stray animals; learning to love a tall, quiet man with Slavic cheekbones, laughing eyes, and lips that could destroy a woman forever.

For her own peace of mind she had to go now, before she talked herself into believing that just because she'd discovered all that, she could lay claim to it. As it was, she was taking with her something of infinite value: a quiet core of stability and warmth that had been entirely missing from her old world.

Not to mention a few lessons in practicality. From now on when she shopped, Chloe was going to be a reader of fabric labels. Almost every stitch she owned required dry cleaning—including her two best night-gowns!

After studying the map Buster had provided along with a full tank of gas to assuage his guilty conscience, she had opted to continue on Highway 17, which tied into I-95 near Fredericksburg, rather than turn west toward Rocky Mount and take the newer interstate all the way up. It looked as if 17 would be much more interesting, and besides, having repeatedly failed to reach Ginny, Chloe was beginning to have strong second thoughts about barging in on her unannounced.

What would be wrong with trying her luck in some nice small town along the way? She'd passed through any number of them, a few of them little more than neighborhoods scattered along the highway. She liked the climate; she liked the people. And there was nothing that dictated she couldn't move on again if the mood struck her.

Three thousand dollars would buy her very little time. Room and board, perhaps, but little in the way of training. And training was an absolute necessity. Who wanted to hire a woman who could do absolutely nothing, no matter how beautifully she did it?

She could arrange flowers but that didn't make her a florist. She could plan a meal for any number of people and oversee it to perfection, but that didn't make her a chef. She could—

On the other hand, the chef wasn't the only one who worked in a restaurant. If she could get a job in some nice eating establishment as hostess, waitress—or perhaps she could even learn to operate a cash register; it couldn't be that difficult—then at least she could be reasonably sure of having one meal a day. How much training could it take to cart trays of food and dirty dishes back and forth from the kitchen?

"Palmer, hustle your butt and clear number four, pick up that order for number seven, and this time, remember to give them the check before they leave!"

On the other hand, perhaps something in interior decorating...

Five hours later, Chloe had left Gumtree Corners and North Carolina far behind. Out of sight, out of mind, she kept telling herself. But it wasn't working. Nor had she really expected it to.

Was he still at the office? Or had he brought Janet home with him, now that they could be alone? Had he confessed how close they had come to making love this morning?

Probably. Quint was nothing if not honest.

Had he assured her that it had meant nothing?

No. He wouldn't have told Janet that, because it *had* meant something. For both of them. Chloe knew Quint, and the depth of her knowing more than made up for its lack of breadth. Neither he nor she was the type to indulge in casual sex. He was the only man besides her husband she had ever come close to sleeping with.

And, small-minded or not, she hoped the memory of what she and Quint had shared would stick in his mind like a burr, long after he and Janet had settled into a comfortable rut.

Which was a totally, unforgivably selfish thought.

Speeding past small scattered farmhouses and rolling brown hills Chloe asked herself for the hundredth time, "Why couldn't I have found him first?"

She had never liked the answer that came to her, nor did she this time. Even if she had found him first, it would never have worked. A man like Quint needed a woman who... He needed...

Well, at the very least, he needed a woman capable of doing more than shopping, arranging his social calendar and being gracious to his friends and business associates. She couldn't even give him a baby, she thought bitterly—not unless some minor medical miracle took place.

Oh, for heaven's sake, now she'd gone and melted her mascara, and it was stinging her eyes, and the only thing in sight was a grease pit of a service station that probably didn't even have a ladies' room!

Still, she'd better stop. This chrome-bedecked barge of hers had a voracious appetite—something Buster had failed to mention. She'd be better off to trade it in on a bicycle once she got settled.

"Ten dollars' worth, please." Gone were the days of credit cards and "Fill it up."

"Yes'm. Check unner th' hood, ma'am?"

"Yes, please." She would have given half of all she owned for an inkling of what was supposed to be under there and just how it was supposed to work. Neither Hollins nor the school in Switzerland she'd attended had taught a course in automotive maintenance. "And may I please have the key to the ladies' room?"

"Ain't locked. Just go on 'round behind the compressor. You'll see it." He pointed a filthy finger, which gave her some indication of where and what a compressor was, and she hurried away.

Five minutes later, having held a damp paper towel over her eyes until she resembled a raccoon and then repaired the damages, Chloe hurried back out to her car and paid the tab, begrudging every penny of it.

Funny—she'd never before resented spending money, but it seemed almost sinful to squander so much on the very thing that was carrying her farther and farther away from where she wanted to be.

Besides, it was such an ugly car. What wasn't covered with rust, bumper stickers or peeling chrome was the exact same color of the overcooked string beans she'd had for lunch. Which was better, she supposed, than being the color of the meat loaf that had accompanied them. Fortunately, both had tasted better than they had looked.

Not even waiting for the attendant to wrap her bill around the greasy wad in his pocket, Chloe switched on the ignition.

Nothing happened.

Peering through the cracked green steering wheel, she checked the position of the gear lever and tried it again, but not so much as a whimper erupted from under the faded green hood. "I beg your pardon, but did you finish checking my—whatever it was you were checking?" she asked the hovering garageman, thinking that perhaps he had left something switched off that was supposed to be switched on.

"Yes'm. You could use another quart o' oil, but I didn't want to do nothing without astin' first."

Oil. That sounded rather critical. For his end of the deal, she would have expected Buster to leave her in better shape than this. "Then perhaps you'd better—"

"What's wrong, Chloe? Problems?"

A sack of concrete landing on her chest could have had no greater impact. She hadn't even seen him drive up. When her heart had slowed down enough so that she could catch her breath, Chloe said, "My oil— It won't start. I'm sure it's nothing that can't be fixed."

"I'm sure, too," he replied, and with a level look at the station attendant, who seemed inordinately interested in a stack of old tires, Quint raised the hood and peered inside. A moment later, she saw him reach in with one hand. The broad shoulder muscles flexed once or twice under a layer of navy plaid flannel, and then he slammed the hood down and directed, "Try it now."

It started purring instantly.

"That's wonderful! What did you—"

"Get out. Leave it running, put it in Park and get out, Chloe."

From the tone of his voice, Chloe didn't know whether the thing was going to explode, take off like a rocket, or collapse in a rusty heap. All she knew was that she lacked the courage to argue with a man whose eyes had the power to slice through diamonds. She thought she'd seen him angry before, but it was nothing to the way he was now. Pale under his perennial tan, with a harsh patch of color slashed across each angular cheekbone, he was glaring over her head directly at the poor shuffling creature in the greasy coveralls.

"Out!"

"Who, h-him or me?" she stammered.

At the sound of her hesitant voice, he leaned down and brushed a strand of hair from her forehead, his diamond-slicing eyes gone strangely soft again. "You, Chloe. Please."

Without another word, she shifted into Park and slid out, still not knowing what to expect.

Quint turned back to the attendant. "You want to watch that kind of thing, boy," he said in a voice that was deadly quiet. "I've heard of guys getting into serious trouble over stunts like that."

"I didn't do nothing," the man whined.

After one long, hard look, Quint turned and tossed Chloe the keys to his car. "You drive mine, I'll take this tank of yours, just to be sure something else didn't fall off besides a battery connection. There's a motel about three miles back. I'll meet you in the parking lot."

"But, I'm not—"

"Just do it, dammit!"

Just do it, dammit! The words kept repeating themselves in her head as Chloe sped along the highway, scowling at the late-day glare on the windshield. What had got *him* so riled up? She was the one the mechanic had been trying to rip off. And doing a very fine job of it, thanks to her abysmal ignorance.

She glanced in her rearview mirror and saw two tractor trailers and a red Honda. Where the devil was he, anyway? Probably searching through her baggage for stolen towels and silverware.

She almost missed the turnoff to the motel. Tires squealing, she whipped into the parking lot and braked, circling around to face the highway. Perhaps he wasn't coming. Perhaps her bean-green limousine was a valuable collectors' model, and he—

Oh, for pity's sake, her hands were sweaty! She had a good mind to walk out onto the highway and hitch a ride—let him call the highway patrol. Let him send a tow truck for his car.

Oh, yes, she could see the headlines now... *Embezzler's Daughter, Widow Of Bigamist Senator, Sought In Three-State Area For Car Theft.*

By the time her green car lurched into the parking lot and pulled into the space beside her, Chloe's anger had drained away, leaving only a bone-deep weariness.

Quint didn't bother with formalities. "Come on, I could do with something to eat. How about you?"

She hesitated, unwilling to put herself under his spell again.

"Okay, if you'd rather talk here, we can do it. But I warn you, I haven't had anything to eat all day, and that doesn't do a whole lot for my disposition."

Reluctantly Chloe got out and allowed him to lead her into the restaurant, but she avoided the protective hand he placed on the small of her back.

"How did you find me?"

"Easy. Buster said you were hitting 17, trying to make Fredericksburg before dark. All I had to do was drive like a bat out of hell, scan every possible stop along the way, and get lucky. Didn't take more'n half a dozen years off my life. Watch that curb, huh?"

"I see it, thank you."

He grunted and cast her a sidelong look under glowering brows.

The room was nearly full, but Quint had no trouble securing them a table in a secluded area. Chloe slipped into her seat, uncomfortably aware of being rumpled, bedraggled, frizzled and shiny—of slacks, sweater, hair and nose, respectively.

Besides which, she'd probably done a lousy patch-up job on her eye makeup, so now he would know she'd been crying off and on all day.

Thank goodness for dim lighting. If only she could hold up for another thirty minutes.... Sighing, she stiffened her shoulders and waited for Quint to begin. When he didn't, she started to fidget with her fork. "Well, say something!" she finally snapped when the tension got too much for her. They might as well have been the only two customers in the restaurant.

"I kind of thought you might want to say something."

"Me! You're the one who came chasing after me, ordering me around."

"You're the one who took off after promising me you wouldn't."

"I promised you no such thing! I told you I was leaving today—I even told you goodbye last night, if you'd bother to think back."

His lids seemed to lower just a fraction, giving him a deceptively sleepy look. Or an outrageously sexy one. "That was last night. What about this morning?"

"Well, what about it?"

"What'll it be, folks? We got some mighty fine trout, you c'n have it broiled or fried."

"Fine, make it two of them," Quint said without even looking up.

Chloe watched a muscle jerk at the corner of his mouth, causing his mustache to twitch ever so slightly.

"Fried or broiled?"

"Fried." His eyes took in every detail of her appearance, and Chloe felt like apologizing. She'd never in her life had to apologize for her appearance—except for the time she'd spilled the tomato bisque.

"French fries, baked potato?"

"Fries!" Quint replied tersely. *Just wait—sooner or later we'll be alone, and you have some explaining to do, lady.*

"Slaw or tossed salad?"

Quint's patience snapped. "Look, I don't care if you bring us the whole damned pasture to graze, just bring us *something*!"

"Yes, *sir*! And what'll you have to drink with your pasture?"

Chloe came to his rescue out of consideration for the state of his blood pressure. "Iced tea for the gentleman, coffee for me, cream for the coffee, sugar for the tea. Thank you very much for your patience, and we'll both have broiled fish and the green salad with oil-and-vinegar dressing and a dash of Parmesan, please."

Quint tugged at his collar, which was already open. He looked harried. In spite of the forty-four-degree weather outside, he'd left his jacket in his car, and now he looked almost feverish.

"I think you might be catching a cold," Chloe remarked as soon as the waitress had left.

His eyes snapped fire at her. "Do you have the slightest idea of how I felt when I came home and found you were gone?" he demanded, emphasizing every word.

Chloe swallowed and stroked the handle of the fork. "Relieved?" He flinched as if she'd struck him, and she shook her head. "Quint, I honestly thought I was doing the best thing. I still do."

"For which one of us? For you? You get a kick out of dropping in on some poor clod and turning his whole life upside down and then waving your fingers at him and skipping out? Well, you picked the wrong clod this time, honey!"

"Don't call yourself that!"

"Why? Doesn't it appeal to your refined sensibilities? Tough!"

"Why are you doing this? Why did you follow me?" she whispered, and then could only stare at him strickenly while the waitress served them iced tea and coffee and made a production of bringing a pitcher and a carafe for refills.

"Look, can we skip the discussion until after dinner? The way I'm feeling right now, I'm not sure I can handle two things at once without resorting to violence."

Chloe lowered her eyes, but not before she'd seen the look of anguish on Quint's face. She tried to tell herself it was anger. Or it was hunger, or poor lighting. It was anything except what she so desperately wanted it to be.

"Yes, perhaps that would be best," she answered quietly.

They managed to get through the meal without discussing anything more threatening than Urk and Poor Darling, and the likelihood of all the birds leaving if a strange dog took up residence there.

"I thought maybe we could see if Sonny wanted a companion. His wife died a couple of years ago, and his kids are all grown and moved away. I think the old guy gets lonesome—not that he'd ever admit it."

Chloe must have made some suitable response. Finally, they were outside again. It had grown dark and the temperature had dropped several more degrees. Chloe wrapped her arms around herself and shivered in her inadequate silk pantsuit.

Quint came up behind her so close she could feel his warmth, and unconsciously, she moved a step closer. "Look, I'm going to get a room," he said. "We can rest up, do some talking, and then, if we want to, take off again. You got any problems with that?"

Beyond words at that point, Chloe shook her head. For better or worse, they were far from finished.

"All the comforts of home," he commented a short while later. The room had two double beds and the usual array of furnishings. Quint took the ice bucket outside and returned a few minutes later with ice and two ginger ales.

Chloe had already confronted herself in the ruthless light of the bathroom. She shuddered to think that she'd been seated across the table from him for the past hour, looking like this. Her face had lost all its color, her hair was coming down, and her eyes looked as if she'd cried oceans, instead of only rivers.

"Want to watch *Matlock*? He's on in five minutes."

She turned away from the mirror and shook her head. "I think we'd better get this over with, don't you?"

"That sounds pretty fatal."

He was smiling that one-sided smile that lifted his bushy mustache, but his eyes had the look of old, remembered pain. The grooves that deepened when he laughed, or when he was tired, were more pronounced than ever, tonight; and Chloe wanted nothing more than to take his face in her hands and kiss each line, kiss the tiny crow's-feet that bracketed his tired eyes, and then kiss that wonderful, stern, tender mouth of his.

"Quint, I've always considered honesty the best policy."

Honesty! That's a laugh! Your whole life up to now has been one big lie!

"All right, I'll go along with that," Quint rumbled. "You want to go first, or shall I get this meeting under way?"

Chloe dropped down on one of the room's two chairs, her arms dangling at her sides. "Let me, if you don't mind. I just want to say what I have to say and then, if you want me to, I'll leave. Or at least get another room for the night. Right now, I don't think I could make it across the parking lot."

Quint nodded, and she drew a deep breath and plunged in at the middle. The beginning could come later, if it came at all. "I don't know if you remember a news story a while back about State Senator Brice Palmer of Florida who was killed in a plane crash off

Bimini." She waited for a reaction, and when Quint nodded, she went on. "Brice was my husband. At least, until he was killed, I thought he was."

She forced herself to look directly at him while she explained about Sheila Warden, the woman who, immediately after the news of Brice's death, had come forth with a four-year-old son and claimed to be his common-law wife, dating from before he had married Chloe. "Of course, in a case like that, with a child involved, the law isn't very helpful. And Brice was a lawyer—I can't believe he didn't know what a mess he had created."

"I don't suppose he expected to get caught—at least not the way he did. Did you—love him?"

She could tell nothing from Quint's expression. What was he feeling? Pity? Disgust? "I thought I did—at least I think that's what I thought. You see, my father was a rather domineering man, and I've never been particularly assertive. Daddy picked him out for me—or me for him—I'm not sure which. At any rate, I married Brice in good faith. It wasn't a very good marriage, but I don't suppose either of us worked very hard to make it better. If I could have had a baby—"

The doctors had said it was possible, but unlikely; and Brice hadn't been particularly interested in having children. He'd put her off, and of course she'd had no way of knowing he already had a son.

Staring intently at a good reproduction of a bad painting on the motel-room wall, Chloe waited for a comment. When none was forthcoming, she went on. "If you read newspapers at all, or watch the news, I suppose you know that the whole thing ended like a soap opera. Full media coverage of all the sordid details." She managed a shaky laugh. "At first I thought about changing my name and having plastic surgery done on my face, but I've always been a coward when it comes to pain."

A coward when it came to being alone and in pain, at least. It had happened more than a few times since her mother had died. She'd suffered everything from menstrual cramps to migraines.

Quint cleared his throat. Then he got up and filled two glasses with ice. He poured ginger ale over both and brought her one, taking his seat on the edge of the bed nearest her instead of returning to his chair. No word was spoken during those few moments, yet Chloe felt oddly comforted by the small gesture.

"And since then?" he prompted gruffly. "That's been a couple of years, hasn't it?"

"The crash was just over two years ago, but Daddy—committed suicide this past Labor Day Friday. When the bank opened on Tuesday, news of what he'd done was out. The bank examiners were swarming all over our house even before his funeral was over."

Quint was silent for a long while, but sometime during the telling, he had covered her hand with his. Not for the first time, Chloe sat quietly and waited for whatever would come next.

"Were you not aware of the existence of your husband's common-law wife at the time you married him, Mrs. Palmer?"

"Were you aware of your father's reasons for making so many trips to Switzerland, Mrs. Palmer?"

"Did your husband ever brag to you about having a son?"

"Didn't your father's life-style take a turn for the better just two years ago, Mrs. Palmer? Did he tell you where he got the money to buy the house in St. Thomas? Did he tell you—?"

Chloe covered her face with her hands. This time she lacked the pain-dulling numbness that had got her through all the questions before.

"Chloe? Honey, what is it? You don't have to tell me anything, you know—I know all I need to know about you." When she failed to respond, Quint breathed a soft profanity and gathered her into his arms. "There, sweetheart, let it all go," he crooned, pulling her onto his lap. "Don't dam it up. Let it out."

"I d-despise weepy women," she sniffled. "Don't look at me, I'm all red and puffy. I'll be all right in a minute."

"No, you go right ahead. Cry as long as you want to. I never catch cold from sitting around in a wet shirt. Honest."

She sniffled, laughed a little and wiped her eyes on his collar. "You know, it's odd—all through the years since Brice died, and before, when I knew my marriage wasn't working and thought it must be my fault, I never cried. Not once. I don't know what happened—it must be something in the air up here. Maybe I'm allergic to Carolina pines."

"We're in Virginia, but I'm in no mood to quibble over details. Now—anything else you want to get off your chest? I'm still in my listening mode."

Reaching up, Chloe pulled the remaining pins from her tumbled hair. After decades of consciously using flawless grooming as armor, she no longer found it necessary. "Last chance, hmm?"

"Nope. Not by a long shot, I just want you to feel comfortable. I don't want you carrying around a load of stuff that ought to be thrown out with the trash. You cleaned house for me—let me return the favor."

"In that case, I may as well confess all my sins. That way, when I leave here I can start with a clear conscience and a clean slate."

"Uh-oh, this sounds serious."

"Not really. But you may as well know that I've been stupid enough to fall in love with you." Before he could utter a word, she hastened to reassure him. "There's absolutely no responsibility on your part, you understand, but as long as I'm confessing, you might as well know that I envy you your home and your rooster and your pigeons—but most of all, I envy Janet with all my heart. She deserves to get what she wants, after growing up in the shadow of a younger sister, but all the same, I wish what she wanted wasn't you."

There. It was said, and her eyes were dry, and in a minute or two, she might even be able to look him in the face and smile.

The room suddenly grew silent. Not even the sound of traffic could be heard for a long moment. "That it? My turn? Good. It's about time we got a few things sorted out here."

Chloe felt as if she could hardly breathe. The neck of her sweater was strangling her, and she pushed herself off his lap and crossed to the single armchair in the room. Keeping her face as expressionless as possible, she waited.

And waited.

"Well? I thought you had something to tell me," she said finally.

"I do. I'm just trying to figure out how a woman can go through all you've been through and still be as dumb as you are."

"I *beg* your—"

"Don't bother. I think we agreed not to stand on ceremony here, so if it's all the same to you, I'll just say what I have to say straight out and let the chips fly."

"By all means," she managed with the last wisp of breath in her lungs. She didn't know which was injured more—her heart or her pride.

"In the first place, I'm no Romeo. I reckon you figured that out for yourself, though. Janet and I— that is, we sort of teamed up by default. Neither of us had anyone else in mind, and it seemed like a pretty fair idea at the time."

Chloe felt her hands and feet growing colder by the moment, but she didn't dare get up and adjust the thermometer—not with Quint glaring at her as if she were a rabbit and he a hawk.

"It turned out to be a lousy idea. Things started going haywire for me the minute I pulled you out of that car. You were like something I dreamed up a long, long time ago, only I didn't know you were real. It had been so long since I'd dreamed at all, I almost didn't recognize you. But I guess instinct takes over when intellect breaks down. And mine did—at least where you were concerned."

Chloe felt the first wisp of hope begin to take shape. "Under the circumstances," she began, when he cut her off.

"No interruptions, right? I'm finding it tough enough to say what I want to say without having to argue about it."

The shadow of a smile brightened her face, and she stared at the hands that were clenched tightly in her lap. Was he saying what she thought he was saying? Could it really be possible that—

"The thing is, I couldn't move ahead without going back and mending my fences. Janet didn't deserve to be dumped. On the other hand, I couldn't see going through with the marriage when I was so damned crazy about you, I didn't know whether I was coming or going."

The smile widened until her cheeks almost hurt, and Chloe dared to look up at him.

Quint groaned. "Ahhh, honey, don't look at me that way, or we'll never get out of this place! Come here—!"

She did. Not content to allow her to sit beside him, Quint lifted her onto his lap again, and Chloe rested her head on his shoulder. "Are you trying to say you love me?"

"What do you think I've been saying all this time? Why do you think I've been acting like a two-headed jackass? Of course I love you, woman! So much that I'm not sure I can function if I can't take you back home with me and keep you there for the next fifty or sixty years."

She closed her eyes and breathed in the powerful aphrodisiac of his scent. "We don't have much in common," she said, feeling compelled to bring a modicum of reason to what struck her as almost unreasonable, impossible, unbearable joy.

"What are you talking about? We have onions and olives and anchovies in common. We have friends and animals in common."

"Urk and Poor Darling?"

"Sonny and Janet and the pigeons. Doc McCall. Buster. The lady who works at The Food Lion who asked me if you were a movie star or something."

Chloe giggled and Quint slowly toppled over backward, carrying her with him. "None of this makes sense, you know. I can't even begin to tell you all the things I don't know how to do."

"So let's start with the things you do know how to do," he replied softly, and within minutes, she had a very good idea of what he had in mind. "I can teach you anything you need to know. I promise I'll devote the rest of my life to instructing you in the art of being Mrs. Quinton Stevens."

"Does that include housekeeping?" she asked as her sweater was pulled off over her head.

"We'll hire someone. You can tell her what you want done, and sit back and look pretty while she does it."

Chloe frowned as she concentrated on the buttons at the front of Quint's navy plaid shirt, one of which had been sewn on with pink thread. "Not on your life, Mr. Y. I got a taste of power last week. I'm going to resurrect that old house of yours and put a shine on it that'll rock you back on your heels!"

Quint lifted her feet up onto the bed and came down beside her again, his eyes slumberous under heavy lids.

"Can we talk about housekeeping later? Right now I've got more important things in mind. And I need your complete attention."

Which he had. Then and an hour later, and six hours later, when they awoke in the middle of the night to make love again.

Over breakfast, which Quint ordered delivered to their room—much to the disgust of the manager, who tried to insist that they didn't offer room service— Chloe learned the details of what had happened with Janet.

"I could've sold her all my stock instead of just a portion, but she's a smart woman. I might not like the direction she'll be taking, but I don't doubt for one minute she'll make a go of it—especially with Adamson as a silent partner."

"So she'll take over your company and you'll start all over again? That hardly seems fair." Chloe reached for a sausage from Quint's plate and munched on it thoughtfully.

"Fair enough. I'm taking over all residential contracts as of the first of the year, and with the capital from the sale, I expect to be in better shape than ever. If you get a hankering to get involved, I could use a woman's viewpoint. If not, there are people who specialize in decorating model houses."

"You say John Adamson's going to go in with Janet?"

Quint leaned over and took the last bite of sausage from her fingertips and then began licking them off, one by one. "Yep," he said between nibbles. "She finally got him eating from the palm of her hand—and you know how helpless a man is when a woman does that to him."

Chloe shuddered as delicious tremors raced down her body. She was limp with satisfaction, in all the ways that counted; but at this rate... "You keep that up, and we'll be here all day."

"You got a problem with that?" Quint buried a kiss in her palm and closed her fingers over it, his dark eyes smiling at her from close range.

"Noooo, not really." Her voice was at least half an octave higher than normal. "But I'd much rather continue this discussion at home, wouldn't you?"

"I thought you'd never ask," he answered in a gravelly drawl. "I'll send Buster up after his car. I'm not letting you out of my sight for the next few years."

"What do you mean, Buster's car? That bean-green limousine is mine, bought and paid for."

He hoisted one eyebrow and grinned. "If you say so, but me, I'd rather drive a parade float."

"So maybe I like parade floats," she said, and maybe she did, at that. All she knew was that there was no more reason to hide—no more reason to run. No matter where she happened to be, as long as Quint was with her, she was finally home for good.

*　*　*　*　*

SILHOUETTE·INTIMATE·MOMENTS®

Premiering this month, a captivating new cover for Silhouette's most adventurous series!

Every month, Silhouette Intimate Moments sweeps you away with four dramatic love stories rich in passion. Silhouette Intimate Moments presents love at its most romantic, where life is exciting and dreams do come true.

Look for the new cover this month, wherever you buy Silhouette® books.

2IMNC-1A

 *Silhouette Books*®

From *New York Times* **Bestselling author**
Penny Jordan, a compelling novel of ruthless passion
that will mesmerize readers everywhere!

Penny Jordan

Silver

Real power, true power came from
Rothwell. And Charles vowed to have it,
the earldom and all that went with it.

Silver vowed to destroy Charles, just as surely and
uncaringly as he had destroyed her father; just as he had
intended to destroy her. She needed him to want her . . .
to desire her . . . until he'd do anything to have her.

But first she needed a tutor: a man who wanted no one.
He would help her bait the trap.

**Played out on a glittering international stage,
Silver's story leads her from the luxurious comfort of
British aristocracy into the depths of adventure,
passion and danger.**

AVAILABLE IN OCTOBER!

 HARLEQUIN

Double your reading pleasure this fall with two Award of Excellence titles written by two of your favorite authors.

Available in September

DUNCAN'S BRIDE
by Linda Howard
Silhouette Intimate Moments #349

Mail-order bride Madelyn Patterson was nothing like what Reese Duncan expected—and everything he needed.

Available in October

THE COWBOY'S LADY
by Debbie Macomber
Silhouette Special Edition #626

The Montana cowboy wanted a little lady at his beck and call—the ''lady'' in question saw things differently....

These titles have been selected to receive a special laurel—the Award of Excellence. Look for the distinctive emblem on the cover. It lets you know there's something truly wonderful inside! DUN-1

Win 1 of 10 Romantic Vacations and Earn Valuable Travel Coupons Worth up to $1,000!

Inside every Harlequin or Silhouette book during September, October and November, you will find a PASSPORT TO ROMANCE that could take you around the world.

By sending us the official entry form available at your favorite retail store, you will automatically be entered in the PASSPORT TO ROMANCE sweepstakes, which could win you a star-studded London Show Tour, a Carribean Cruise, a fabulous tour of France, a sun-drenched visit to Hawaii, a Mediterranean Cruise or a wander through Britain's historical castles. The more entry forms you send in, the better your chances of winning!

In addition to your chances of winning a fabulous vacation for two, valuable travel discounts on hotels, cruises, car rentals and restaurants can be yours by submitting an offer certificate (available at retail stores) properly completed with proofs-of-purchase from any specially marked PASSPORT TO ROMANCE Harlequin® or Silhouette® book. The more proofs-of-purchase you collect, the higher the value of travel coupons received!

For details on your PASSPORT TO ROMANCE, look for information at your favorite retail store or send a self-addressed stamped envelope to:

PASSPORT TO ROMANCE
P.O. Box 621
Fort Erie, Ontario L2A 5X3